knows a thing or two about traps and machines

talen
maste

CO
BLAZE

trickster

(nearly) always keeps his cool

THiLO

Adventure Academy of Europe

The Fire Tiger of Batavia

MIX
Papier | Fördert gute Waldnutzung
FSC® C022120
Mineralöl freie Druckfarbe

5 4 3 2 1

ISBN: 978-3-649-64346-3

Based on an idea of Michael Mack, Jörg Ihle,
Nils Feigenwinter, Tobias Mundinger
Original title: Die fliegende Schule der Abenteurer –
Der Feuertiger von Batavia
Text by THiLO
Translation by Marielle Sutherland
Illustration and Design by Max Meinzold
Edits by Emma Roberts, Sara Falke, Anja Fislage
Layout by Helene Hillebrand, Bielefeld
Printed in Slovakia

www.coppenrath.de

THiLO

ACE

ADVENTURE ACADEMY OF EUROPE

The Fire Tiger of Batavia

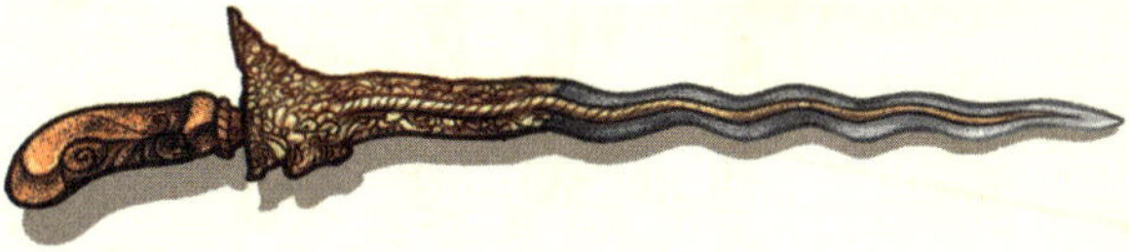

Translated by Marielle Sutherland

With illustrations by Max Meinzold

COPPENRATH

ACE

Prologue:
A Decision With Consequences

Professor Severin Maximov banged the table with the flat of his hand.

"No!"

The white-haired professor was shaking from head to toe in agitation, a swollen vein protruding from his forehead.

The other three men in the room were taken aback. They had never seen the director of the Adventure Club of Europe Academy lose his temper quite like this before.

Catherine Noir was the only person present who didn't bat an eyelid.

"Yes!" she replied, calmly but firmly.

Severin Maximov leapt up with such force that he knocked his chair to the floor.

"Arrgggh! How can anyone be so stubborn?" he railed. "If you're not careful, you will go down in history, my dear! Catherine Noir, the twenty-second president of the

ACE, who, despite many warnings, had the club's most valuable artefact stolen from right under her nose."

He banged the table again. "Reckless! Obstinate! Downright… stupid!"

Catherine Noir stood up and went to the window. Deep Fog Castle's park was shrouded in darkness. All that was visible was the outline of trees against the moon. She was used to people saying harsh things about her. When it came to missing ships, sunken cities or rumours of alien life-forms, every club member tried to persuade the president they needed an expedition – and sometimes this involved her putting up with insults when they didn't get their way. In secret, Catherine Noir was actually delighted by the adventurers' passion – it was precisely this fire, burning in all members, that had held the club together since 1716. Severin Maximov, however, now thought the existence of ACE was under threat.

Noir turned back to the men.

"The new school year begins in seven days' time," she replied. "The climax of the welcome party is always the presentation of the legendary Fire Tiger dagger – and this year will be no exception!"

Severin Maximov looked like he was about to tear his hair out. "The Fire Tiger is more than just a golden dagger, Madame! It is the symbol of our club! It was through the Fire Tiger that our founder Bartholomeus van Robbemond was transformed from a pirate into a collector and protector of unique artefacts. If it were to be stolen…"

Now Mads-Arnor Helmstad joined in the conversation. The Norwegian was tall and gaunt with a shaggy straw-blonde beard and dishevelled hair. All this made him look like a birch tree that had just survived a hurricane.

"Catherine, my source is entirely reliable," he implored the president. "The intention is to steal the dagger. None other than the Masked Phantom has been given the task…"

Severin Maximov bent down to his briefcase and reappeared with a pile of international newspapers. He dumped them down on the table as if he was planning a campfire.

"There you go!" he bellowed scornfully. "Paris, London, New York – their reputation has even reached as far as the Sudan!"

The notorious master thief had indeed made it onto the front covers of most of these newspapers. This time, following the audacious theft of a van Gogh painting from a museum in Amsterdam. Just as after every successful break-in, here too the Phantom was waving brazenly at the security camera – with their famous panther mask over their face, of course.

"Catherine..." droned Dr Helmut Martinsberger with the calming voice of a lion tamer. "In the vault, the Fire Tiger is safe. In the great hall, however..."

Maximov and Helmstad nodded.

But Catherine Noir gave the newspapers nothing more than a cursory glance.

"Do I have to remind you who we are?" she bawled at the men. "For over three hundred years, the members of the Adventure Club of Europe have been investigating and discovering the secrets and mysteries of this world. From the depths of Loch Ness to the peaks of the Himalayas – no amount of risk or danger has ever stopped the brave men and women of the ACE. And now we're supposed to bow down to a thief in a leopard mask?"

"Panther..." Helmstad corrected her gingerly. "The Phantom wears a panther mask..."

Noir took no notice of him.

"The Eulenstein brothers, for example – explorers of the skies. Or Ursula Weber – inventor of the first android. Or our founding father, Bartholomeus van Robbemond – they all believed in the unbelievable, the inconceivable." Suddenly, Noir banged the table too. "I won't let any of today's members crawl off like rabbits into their holes. So the Phantom wants to pay us a visit? Well then, let's send an invitation!"

Now a man in an armchair, who hadn't contributed anything to the discussion so far, cleared his throat. Harold Godric McFinnegan was a teacher of cartography and geomancy – and a Scotsman. As per the reputation of his fellow countrymen, McFinnegan was a man of few words.

"Scots aren't afraid of anything or anyone," he growled grumpily.

Noir smiled. "Then we do everything the way we've always done! My vote counts as triple!"

Maximov threw his arms in the air repeatedly, spluttering with rage. Then he turned on his heel and left the room. The other men followed him.

Catherine Noir was left alone. "There's an opportunity in every crisis…" she murmured, tucking the newspapers away into her drawer.

Before closing the drawer again, her eyes fell on one of the photos of the Phantom in the panther mask. The Phantom smiled back at her, as if they were looking forward to their showdown with the ACE.

Guests From All Over the World

Belle Pompadour was sitting in the passenger seat of a black vintage car that was racing down a narrow road at one hundred miles per hour, enjoying a strong headwind. As the car sped along, she kept checking the sun visor mirror. This morning, back in London, she'd had a pink streak dyed into her blonde hair. She hadn't got used to it yet. She pushed the mirror up again. There was even less chance she'd ever get used to her dad's stubbornness. The roads were getting narrower and bumpier – but Pierre Pompadour simply refused to install a satnav.

"Papa," she admonished him. "Are we really going the right way? I haven't seen a single road sign for a quarter of an hour." They hadn't passed any houses, never mind people, for ages.

Pierre Pompadour grinned and pushed down harder on the accelerator. Belle sighed and looked out of the window. She was as excited as… as… well, as she should be on the first day of school. So far, her family had had absolutely nothing to do with the ACE. The club's attention had only been drawn to Belle when, after a failed safari when she was eight years old, she had survived for a week alone in the Sahara. Aside from that, she could now speak eight languages and was an expert in ancient symbols.

Nonetheless, Belle was tense. Would she be able to keep up with all the super-talented kids in the academy? Belle knew that most of the other pupils came from families who had been involved with the Adventure Club of Europe for centuries. Their ancestors had been there when the Egyptian pharaohs were excavated, or had released the last Tasmanian tigers back into the wild in Australia, or had taken part in the first 'unmanned' orbit of the moon (the passengers were exclusively *women*, which Belle found very amusing…).

And Belle? Yes, she had a huge amount of knowledge to offer and she'd also won all the youth fencing tournaments in France. But was that enough?

With squealing tyres, the car did a last-minute swerve onto a dirt track.

"Papa!" Belle yelled, panic-stricken.

"Belle!" her dad replied dismissively, with a patronising smile. "I've always managed to get to wherever I want to go. A modern device like a satnav just wouldn't suit this car."

Belle snorted. "If we get there too late, I'll…"

Pierre Pompadour chewed on the tips of his moustache. Suddenly, the visibility dropped, so he had to reduce his speed to what was, for him, a feeble eighty miles per hour. It was getting foggier by the minute. Soon, Belle could barely see anything at all. They found themselves in front of an old mill. Behind it was nothing but forest.

"Are you sure that's the academy?" Belle asked spikily.

Pierre Pompadour didn't reply. He just spun the steering wheel right round, put the pedal to the metal and raced back in the direction they had come from.

Belle could have strangled him! How could someone be so stubborn? By now they were probably further from Deep Fog Castle than from the moon! Although, the current fog at least seemed fitting.

Belle was thrown around as her dad swerved onto a side road. Beeping the horn, he overtook a dirt-encrusted off-road vehicle with a tent strapped to the roof, then jostled past a shiny sports car. And suddenly, there it was. As if out of nowhere, the castle rose up from the dense fog it was named after.

Pierre Pompadour zipped under the eight long metal legs of a beetle-like vehicle and out onto the castle forecourt. The limousine braked so hard that it sent gravel spraying in all directions.

Pierre Pompadour held his watch under Belle's nose. "3 p.m. Bang on time, to the second!"

Belle threw open the passenger door and leapt, red-faced, out of the car. "Thanks for the wonderful journey, Papa!" she snapped, slamming the door. She stomped round to the boot and pulled out her duffel bag. "You know what?" she yelled at her dad. "As far as I'm concerned, you can drive back without a satnav too – in fact, you can go right now. I'd like to enjoy the party without you."

And with that, she did an about-turn and stomped off in the direction of a bar table where two teachers were serving cool drinks and cucumber sandwiches.

"Belle!" her dad called after her. "What's wrong?"

But Belle didn't even turn round. A teacher who looked like a tree held his tray out towards her. But she'd lost her appetite. She just wanted to get to her room as quickly as possible.

A queue had formed at the entrance to the castle. What else was Belle to do but join it? An older red-haired, red-bearded man stood at the gate, greeting every newcomer with a handshake. As Belle approached, she recognised him as a teacher she had met at her interview a few months before.

As always, Harold Godric McFinnegan was wearing a three-piece tweed suit, looking exactly as Belle imagined a respectable professor should. By all accounts, he looked nothing like a daring adventurer. But he represented the ACE with old English charm and class – even though, as Belle knew, he was a proud Scotsman.

"He doesn't even take a bath without his tie on," a pupil standing behind Belle whispered.

As Belle arrived at the front of the queue, something that sounded like pistol shots rang out behind the roofs of Deep Fog Castle. Everyone looked up. A peculiar flying machine was curving its way around the towers. It looked like an iron sausage; plumes of black smoke were coming out of three large pipes. The thing did a loop, stopped with a squeal of its brakes in mid-air, then lowered itself to the ground. With a hiss, a hatch opened and a four people climbed out: a man, a woman and two boys. The younger boy looked around, scarlet-faced. The man took off his goggles and pushed the boy towards McFinnegan.

"Harold, how wonderful to see you!" declared the man. "Are you admiring my latest invention? It's an O-boat. The 'O' stands for 'over' – over land, over water, over clouds!"

McFinnegan nodded politely but not enthusiastically.

"May I introduce your new pupil?" the pilot continued. "This is Oli!"

The boy looked down at the floor, embarrassed. "My name is Oliver!" he protested in a squeaky voice. "An 'i' at the end of a name is a diminutive form, given to house pets and the like. But I'm not a kitten, am I?"

"Oliver Snyder – welcome!" McFinnegan greeted the boy. "We've put you in the Machu Picchu room."

Oliver's father clapped his hands. "Ah, wonderful! That was my room too – and your grandmother's!" He laughed, too loudly. "Machu Picchu, Oli. The legendary city of the Inca Empire in the Andes! See, we are born for higher things!"

Oliver Snyder rolled his eyes.

Belle bit her lower lip. Maybe she'd been too harsh with her dad. No matter how embarrassing he was, others apparently had it much much worse…

Then, in the middle of the grounds, an enormous elephant appeared as if out of nowhere. On its back sat a woman who looked to be about ninety years old. She had dark skin and snow-white hair and was wearing countless necklaces. Sat behind her was a girl, clinging on tight and surveying the castle with big wide eyes. Just as curious was the meerkat peering out of the girl's rucksack.

"Oni Amaka," murmured the teacher. "Seems to have inherited her great-grandmother's love of animals..."

The cow elephant wrapped her trunk around her rider and placed her down carefully beside a bed of peppermint. Oni clambered down the folds of the elephant's skin like it was a rope ladder. The meerkat cheered her on with loud

screeching. Barely had they both made it down before the outline of the elephant became a blur and eventually disappeared altogether.

Belle was gobsmacked. She looked around, but none of the other people around her seemed to think this was anything out of the ordinary.

Belle took some deep breaths. On the one hand, she now had an even stronger feeling she wasn't good enough for this academy. On the

other hand, she was eager to hear every single pupil's story.

When she turned to the front of the queue again, a woman was standing next to McFinnegan. She had shoulder-length dark hair and was dressed entirely – and elegantly – in black. Her red lipstick not only accentuated her beauty, it also gave her an air of mystery.

"Belle Pompadour, welcome to Deep Fog Castle," the woman greeted Belle in French. Belle had another reason to like her straightaway. "I'm Catherine Noir, President of the ACE. I believe we two have more in common than just our nationality."

She smiled enigmatically, then looked up at the castle. Behind a window, Belle recognised Severin Maximov, the director of the academy who had invited her for interview in the first place.

"I wonder whether our ghost hunter has already had a sighting of the Phantom?" Noir muttered to McFinnegan.

Then she cleared her throat and turned to the pupils. "Welcome, or rather – welcome back to Deep Fog Castle! First of all, please settle yourselves in your rooms, but make sure you also get to the start-of-year ceremony on time!"

Some of the parents clapped; the pupils either

nodded casually or just went on eating their cucumber sandwiches.

Noir spoke again, but only to Belle and McFinnegan, quietly. “I’m going back to my office. I’ve still got a few things to prepare.”

Belle didn’t have a clue what she meant by this. She listened while McFinnegan gave her directions to her room, which was called Luxor, then dragged her duffel bag up the sweeping stone staircase to the first floor. As soon as she set eyes on the nearest of the four-poster beds inside, Belle suddenly realised how exhausted she was and dropped down onto the deep mattress. It surely couldn’t hurt to have a little nap before the ceremony.

Maybe she shouldn’t have sent her dad home.

“Whatever,” she mumbled into her pillow. “I won’t let you and Mama down.”

And with that, she fell into a deep sleep.

Too Late

Belle woke with a start. She struggled to get her bearings. Where was she? Who was she? And above all, what time was it?

Still fuzzy in the head, Belle Pompadour glanced at the clock on her smartphone.

"Zut alors!" she cried, leaping out of bed. "Zut, zut, zut!"

Belle grabbed her duffel bag and fished out her ceremony dress. She started making a dash for it, pulling off her trousers at the same time. Before she reached the door, she stumbled over a rucksack with a colourful geometric pattern on it – it hadn't been there earlier.

Belle banged her shoulder on the bedpost. That was bound to give her a proper bruise. Fortunately, it wouldn't appear until tomorrow. Pulling her dress on over her head, she staggered into the corridor. Now the stupid thing had got caught on her earring…

Totally disorientated, Belle panted her way along the

corridor. All the other pupils and their families seemed to have left for the ceremonial hall a long time ago. But how was she supposed to find her way there? The castle was an absolute labyrinth!

"Zut alors!" she cursed again.

Finally, she managed to free her dress from the earring. Now she could see again at least. Belle glanced at an enormous wall clock. The ceremony was starting in one minute!

"Left or right?" Belle muttered at the next junction. She was talking to herself – there was no one else around.

"Left to the ceremonial hall," the clock replied.

Belle was startled, but much too agitated to wonder at it.

"Thanks!" she said, running in the suggested direction. Finally! The main entrance hall was ahead of her now – she recognised that from earlier. Belle slowed down.

Two men in old-fashioned uniforms were standing beside a set of enormous double doors. Above them hung an oil painting of Bartholomeus van Robbemond, the founder of the ACE. He was wearing his pirate clothes and big gold ring with pride, smiling in a confident, self-assured way. Belle tried to adopt the same confidence.

But when she was only a few steps from the entrance, the bell rang in the castle chapel. The guards grabbed the handles on the open doors, marched towards each other and eventually disappeared into the hall, closing the doors behind them.

"Stop!" called Belle, still out of breath. "Wait a minute!"

Just as she reached the doors, an orchestra struck up.

I'm in luck! thought Belle. This meant no one would notice her creeping into the hall. But the doors were already locked!

Belle cursed again, and considered her options. This had been the official entrance for kings and dukes and lords. But there must also be a staff entrance. And Belle was going to find it!

She dashed back in the direction she had just come from and turned a different corner at the first junction she came to. The corridor she was running down now was considerably narrower and plainer than the others – there were no paintings on the walls. She must be on the right track! She immediately slowed down and her heart stopped racing.

Suddenly, applause broke out in the distance. A man with a deep growling voice was speaking to the guests. Belle couldn't make out what he was saying, but his voice was louder than the audience's clapping. She reckoned she must be close to the stage. Belle stayed where she was, smoothing down her dress. She had no desire to suddenly find herself emerging onto the stage too, like a rabbit in the headlights, interrupting the ceremony. Belle closed her eyes briefly. Then she hurried round the corner – and collided with something soft. Or rather, with *someone* soft.

"Urrgh," groaned a voice from out of the darkness.

Belle fell backwards, onto the floor. After a brief moment of confusion, she looked up.

The figure before her stood between two pieces of stage set, bent double and pressing his hand against his stomach.

Belle was sure it was a boy. He was a little taller than her and dressed from head to toe in black. He was even wearing a black balaclava, like the ones motorcyclists wear under their helmets. No wonder she hadn't seen him here in the darkness.

He was probably about to do an ACE stunt or something like that. He was surely waiting for his cue.

Belle held out her hand to him. The figure didn't react, but stared at Belle in surprise.

"Well, are you going to help me up, or what?" hissed Belle.

Then there was a flash of lightning behind her. Belle closed her eyes and covered her head with her arms to protect herself. When nothing else happened, Belle opened her eyes again. A little white cloud was suspended in the middle of the corridor.

"W-what was that?" she stammered, looking up. But there was no one there. The figure had vanished. She couldn't hear any steps, either. Only the speech from inside the hall penetrated the silence.

Belle stood up, shook herself, still confused, and walked towards the speaker's voice. Now, the only thing separating her from the ceremonial hall was a thick black curtain. Belle peeped through it. She was only a few metres away from a white-haired man who was strutting across the stage like a peacock. Maximov.

The balaclava boy wasn't with him, and there was no motorbike, either. Apart from the director and a table draped to the floor with a claret-coloured velvet cloth, the stage was empty. Belle crept on tiptoe to the edge of the curtain and waited. Finally, after what felt like an eternity, Maximov took a bow. The audience broke out in thunderous applause. Belle slipped through the curtain at the side of the stage and walked down the steps to the main hall, trying to radiate confidence. If she pretended she was supposed to be coming from backstage, she'd look like it, too, and no one in the audience would think anything of it. This way, she'd be almost invisible…

Belle Pompadour sat down in one of the few empty chairs, joined in the applause, and smiled as if it had been the best speech she'd ever heard in her life. But if Belle had known that Catherine Noir's eyes had been following her every step, she certainly wouldn't have smiled…

A Party Of Surprises

Belle felt the tension evaporating from her body. And she noticed something else: the boy next to her was staring at her unashamedly. He had a neat parting in his hair and metal-rimmed glasses. His shirt was buttoned up all wrong under his old-fashioned sleeveless jumper, and he was slumped in his chair like a wet sack.

Nerd! Belle couldn't help thinking. The kind of boy who plays computer games all night long and wears sandals with socks. She looked down, unable to stifle a giggle.

Wasn't this Oliver? The boy who'd arrived in the flying machine? Bingo – it *was* him!

When Oliver grinned, clearly embarrassed, Belle pulled herself together.

"Have I missed anything important?" she whispered to him.

"Oh, yes!" Oliver gushed. "The choir of teachers and two English folk dances!"

Belle pulled a face. Choir? Folk dances? Really?

"Did you know that the transverse flute is regarded as a woodwind instrument – even though it's made of metal? The first flutes were actually made of bone!"

Belle shook her head, her eyes glazing over.

"I'm… I'm Oliver," the boy introduced himself shyly. "And what's your n—"

"Shh, Oli!" the man beside Oliver reprimanded him.

Oliver hung his head. Belle was pleased the conversation was over. And if she didn't want to keel over with boredom, she'd never start another one with Oliver ever again.

The rest of the ceremony, however, was anything but boring. One by one, the members of the Adventure Club of Europe introduced themselves to the audience and talked about their expeditions and discoveries. An genteel lady played her conversation with an alien over the loudspeaker; the full-bearded man who looked like a tree gave an account of the unfathomable energy of polar rays in the Arctic; and to conclude, an overweight man in a bicycle helicopter hovered over the audience's heads.

Once he'd landed safely, Belle realised how dry her throat was. Had she really sat there the whole time with her mouth gaping wide open? The nerdiness of the boy sitting beside her was clearly starting to rub off.

Then Catherine Noir stepped up to the lectern.

"Welcome, adventurers, teachers, scientists, members of the ACE, pupils," she began. "More than three centuries ago, something extraordinary happened on an Indonesian island. Bartholomeus van Robbemond – who until then had been an ordinary pirate and thief – had had enough of plundering treasure. He carried on hunting for unusual artefacts, magical objects and unexplained phenomena, but not so he could exploit them for his own ends. Quite the opposite. He collected these things in order to preserve them for posterity and stop them falling into the wrong hands – and above all, the hands of his arch-enemy, Diablo Cortez, nicknamed 'The Bull'."

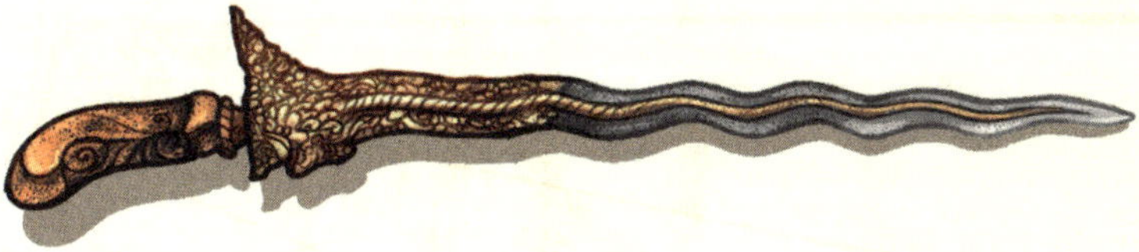

Noir came out from behind the lectern and strode along the edge of the stage.

"Since then, many of these pieces have been stored securely in the vault under your feet. Including the most famous object of all, the object which inspired van Robbemond's conversion and culminated in the founding of the ACE in 1716… the Fire Tiger. A wavy dagger known as a kris, its value is inestimable. Not because of its golden handle. Or the jewels encased within it. It is the magical power of the Fire Tiger that makes it unique. According to the legend, the person who carries it is invincible. Furthermore, as van Robbemond himself wrote in his logbook: 'It is enough to point the blade at someone. This alone will reduce his bones to dust and his hair to ash.'"

The president stood still. "But I have talked for long enough. Now you shall see it with your own eyes. It is released from its cage in the castle cellar only once a year. Ladies and gentlemen, I present to you… the Fire Tiger!"

Belle desperately wanted to clap, but the rest of the guests remained silent, spellbound. The eyes of all five hundred guests were focused on the claret-coloured velvet curtain draped over the table. Finally, it was pulled aside, and the entire audience gasped in unison, as if they were a single living being. An enormous lizard took broad strides onto the stage, down the steps and into the hall. It was a good two metres long – Belle recognised it as a Komodo dragon. Only, it wasn't greenish grey but snow-white. It had to be an albino!

The lizard plodded along the front row of the audience. Flicking its tongue, it swivelled its head from one side to the other. A wooden casket with the ACE logo was lashed to its back, see-sawing up and down with the rhythm of its steps.

"Harry!" the older pupils called out.

"Treat him with respect!" Noir cautioned the academy students. "After all, Harry is already over two hundred and thirty years old."

And he gobbles up live goats in a few bites… Belle thought to herself.

Maybe it was something to do with his advanced years, but the imposing lizard wasn't in the least disturbed by all the commotion around him. Just as he had probably done in previous decades, he headed straight back to the stage and stopped in front of the table.

A woman and man from the audience stood up – going by their collective age, they were probably not much younger than Harry. They followed the lizard on to the stage.

"Like every year, it is the honourable task of the two oldest members of the club to receive the casket from Harry," Noir continued.

The two elderly adventurers put on white gloves and lifted the wooden treasure chest from Harry's back, onto the table.

"However, I shall be the one to open it, for I have the only key… here!"

Catherine Noir reached for a chain that was fastened to her belt and pulled a heavy key out of her pocket. As

she raised the key into the air, two things happened: the guests clapped enthusiastically – and the lights went out in the hall.

Belle wolf-whistled, she was so caught up in this perfectly theatrical presentation of the Fire Tiger – the legend, the lizard, the ancient club members, the key, and now the climax… the darkness.

The guests around Belle cheered and shouted, too. It was only after a few moments that Belle realised the voices did not sound cheerful. Chairs were being tipped over, people were running away, shoving one another. And over the top of everything, she could hear the desperate cries of Catherine Noir.

“Light, we need light immediately!” she roared into the microphone. “And keep the doors locked!”

Only now did it dawn on Belle that the darkness was not at all part of the presentation.

After what seemed like an eternity, there were a few isolated flashes of light. Catherine Noir was still standing on the stage, clasping the key in her hand. In her other hand she was holding a silver pen with a blade protruding from the front of it. She would defend the Fire Tiger to the death – everyone in the hall knew it. But it wouldn’t come to that yet, for the casket on the table beside her was open – and empty. Now Belle’s heart was beating faster, too. The Fire Tiger had been stolen! In front of their very eyes!

"Over here!"

Belle craned her neck. Oliver was standing at the edge of the hall in semi-darkness, in front of the emergency exit. He raised his arm as if he was begging his teacher for urgent permission to go to the toilet.

"Over here!" he called again, in a squeaky voice. "Everyone come over here!"

No one heard him in the pandemonium, but Belle could sense the fear in his voice.

She immediately jostled her way through to him.

By now, Oliver was kneeling down. In front of him, a person with a black balaclava over his head lay curled up on the floor. And peeping out of his rucksack was the handle of the Fire Tiger.

The figure from backstage! They rolled him onto his back and Belle flinched with fear. Two glinting panther eyes were printed on the front of the black mask. The most famous thief in living memory was right in front of them!

"Go on! Pull his mask up!" Oliver urged her.

When Belle didn't react, he stretched out his own fingers towards the Phantom. But right at that moment, the two guards from the doors pulled him off the thief, who was out cold.

"Have you got a death wish, kid?" the larger of the two

barked at Oliver. "You know what will happen if the blade points at you!"

Oliver nodded like a school swot who'd been caught copying answers.

Catherine Noir made her way through the crowd.

"Take him to my office," she commanded. "Bind his arms – and don't let him out of your sight for even a moment. I won't be long."

The guards slung the Phantom's arms over their shoulders and dragged him out of the ceremonial hall.

The president climbed up on a chair.

"Dear guests, please calm down," she urged in a forbidding voice. "We were warned in the run-up to the ceremony that a thief would attempt to steal the Fire Tiger." Catherine Noir smiled. "Well, it will remain just that – an attempt, thanks to an ingenious brainwave from our academy director, Severin Maximov. He daubed the lid of the treasure chest with a contact poison that knocks a person out only a few seconds after touching it. Our oldest club members were briefed on this in advance, which is why they put gloves on first."

Everyone in the hall clapped. Belle and Oliver, however, exchanged disappointed looks. They'd missed the chance to reveal the identity of one of the most famous thieves in the world – and only just.

Where is Everyone?

In the entrance hall of Deep Fog Castle there was only one topic on everyone's lips. Wherever Belle went, everyone was talking about the thwarted theft.

"You really have to admire this Phantom's audacity!" trumpeted Oliver's father, Dick Snyder, at the group he was talking to. Belle stopped to listen. "If he wasn't such a scoundrel, he'd be a worthy member of the ACE."

The people around Mr Snyder protested strongly. Beside him, Oliver was investigating the fascinating physics of drinking through a straw.

Dick Snyder looked at his son, shaking his head in despair. "I wish our Oli had even a modicum of his courage, but unfortunately, he is atypical of our family."

Belle saw Oliver was turning red.

"My name is Oliver, Papa," he squeaked back.

Dick Snyder ruffled his hair. "My boy," he blustered, "I didn't mean it like that. Maximov will make a great adventurer out of you. I'm one hundred per cent certain of this. One day, you will complete the mission your grandmother and I could not: discovering the ruins of Batavia!"

He laid his hand on his son's shoulder. Oliver's face seemed to suggest his father's hand was as heavy as a millstone.

When Oliver looked over at Belle, she turned away quickly. If she talked to him again this evening, the nerd was bound to start thinking she was his friend, and Belle really didn't fancy that at all. If she was going to find proper friends, she'd be wise to stay away from people wearing sleeveless jumpers and socks with sandals.

Belle manoeuvred herself into a crowd of older pupils but they wouldn't even entertain talking to a newcomer, and Belle was much too proud to beg for their attention. So she drank her juice and went up to the first floor. This time, because she wasn't panicking about being late, she found her way easily.

But then she stopped dead in the middle of the corridor. The door to her room, Luxor, was wide open. Belle crept closer. She could hear frantic noises, as if someone was rummaging through her stuff. Alarm bells went off in Belle's head. Had the Phantom broken free again? Was he in there now, trying to crack open her very lean piggy bank? Belle took one big leap into the room.

"What are you doing here?" she called out.

A girl with tight black curls let out a shriek and spun to face the door. An animal was somersaulting around on her arm.

It was the girl who'd arrived on the disappearing elephant!

"Sorry," said Belle. "I didn't want to scare you. But the door..."

The girl smiled, embarrassed. "I don't like being in rooms with closed doors. I always feel like I'm in a cage."

She stopped, then held her hand out towards Belle.

"I'm Oni. We're roommates – or whatever you call it."

Belle took her hand. "I'm Belle. And who is this cute little fellow here?"

She tried prodding the little animal's nose with her finger, but it screeched and hid in Oni's curls.

Oni's face lit up. "This is Anubi, my meerkat. He's not only cute, he's also unbelievably greedy. So don't leave any food around that you want to eat yourself, especially no tasty titbits like scorpions, cockroaches or praying mantises…”

Belle shook her head, laughing. “Okay, I’ll make sure I don’t.” She yawned. “And now I really need to sleep. What a day it’s been!”

Belle fell backwards onto the four-poster bed. She was already asleep before her head hit the pillow.

*

When Belle awoke the next day, she knew straightaway that something wasn't right. The door was gaping wide open, and the bed on the other side of the room was empty and untouched. Oni and Anubi weren't there. Oni's rucksack wasn't there either, and her cupboard was empty. They'd obviously moved out. But why?

Belle wanted to go looking for them, but it was already 7.53 a.m. Breakfast was at eight sharp. Belle didn't want to be late a second time – even though it would only be her who knew it had happened once before. Maybe Oni just wasn't a good sleeper and was already cheerfully munching at the breakfast table.

It was total chaos in the dining hall. There were around forty pupils altogether, and no teachers in sight. Belle couldn't see Oni here either, or Oliver.

Belle got a glass of orange juice and sat down with a few people she recognised.

She remembered that four of them were in her year group. They introduced themselves curtly as Zack, Polly, Akono and Mary-Jay, then didn't pay any further attention to Belle.

"And what's your name?" Belle asked the fifth person at the table. The clique of four were ignoring him too. Was that why he was looking so bad-tempered?

"Connor Blaze," the boy replied gruffly.

Belle wasn't going to be put off by his abrasiveness.

"Were you here yesterday? I didn't see you."

The boy's eyes narrowed to two slits and he shook his head.

"I only arrived this morning, at dawn."

"Tut tut," said Belle, trying to make a joke of it, "you should have brought your parents up better than that!"

"My parents are dead," replied Connor, looking out of the window.

Zut alors! thought Belle. *Now I've put my foot in it!*

"Oh, I'm so—"

Connor stood up. "No need to be sorry. It was over six years ago."

He took his empty bowl and went back to the buffet.

"Well then, I'm even more sorry," muttered Belle.

Just then, the director, Maximov, came into the hall.

Suddenly, the older pupils fell silent – Maximov obviously had a reputation for being strict.

"I'd like to welcome you again myself to the academy of the Adventure Club of Europe," Maximov began. "Our newcomers must have worked out by now that this is no normal school. The subjects you will study bear no comparison with any of the useless knowledge you have been fed in your schooling thus far. Moreover, the lessons, for the most part, will not take place in this building."

Maximov went on to explain that they were all being prepared for a career as adventurers and guardians of magical artefacts, that everyone here stood out from the crowd because they had a special ability, that they could all learn something from one another, and so on.

Suddenly, in the middle of his speech, the door flew open. Two teachers brought in a boy they were almost carrying; he was barely walking for himself. Oliver! He looked bleary-eyed.

"We found him in the engineering room," the teacher who looked like a tree reported to the director. "It looks like he's spent the entire night playing computer games."

"I wasn't gaming!" Oliver protested in his squeaky voice. "I was recoding my character. Now they're invincible!"

There was a glimmer of pride in Oliver's eyes, but it didn't last long. The director's icy gaze was upon him; he fell silent.

"Well, I'm finished explaining things anyway," replied Maximov cantankerously. "So, pack your things, everyone! Your teachers and I will meet you at the airport. Departure is at twelve sharp!"

An older boy on the next table raised his hand.

"Yes, Kasimir?" said Maximov.

"What happened with the thief?"

“Yes, what happened? Is the Phantom still haunting our castle?” another boy sneered.

Maximov’s eyelids flickered. “What do you think happened? We handed him over to the police yesterday.”

A Group of Outsiders

Black clouds hung over the five-hundred-year-old yew trees in the castle grounds. Belle shivered. She was crossing the wooden footbridge that led from the upper floor of the castle, down to the airport. There was a spooky atmosphere – it was much too dark for the time of day, and there was not a soul in sight. This time, she was much too early, and a storm was coming. She hoped they'd still get away on time.

Slowly, the outlines of enormous airships rose up before Belle. The larger ones were hovering between the crowns of the trees, their rope ladders dangling down to the footbridges. The smaller ones were moored like boats to iron rings, rocking gently from side to side. These were Sky Explorers, the supersonic zeppelins that lessons would be held in. Not here at the castle, of course, but during excursions to countries all around the globe.

Thinking about all the journeys they were about

to embark upon was giving Belle butterflies in her tummy. She stopped at the end of the bridge under a low overhanging branch, and waited.

The others pupils began to arrive in dribs and drabs. They all had little suitcases or rucksacks with them. Oliver, however, was puffing and panting, dragging three enormous bags behind him.

"How long are you going away for?" enquired Zack. "Five years?"

The other three members of the clique laughed. Even Belle couldn't suppress a smile, but somehow she felt sorry for Oliver. She gave him a nod of encouragement, which unfortunately Oliver took as an invitation to come over and talk to her.

"That's an Explorer X9-24," he explained to Belle. "It flies up to 1000 miles per hour – that's 1609.34 kilometres per hour, if you prefer the metric system."

Belle took deep breaths. Maybe she could fly away?

"As you must know, the speed of sound is 343.2 metres per second – which is 1,236 kilometres per hour. Which means…"

Belle tapped him on the shoulder. "Oliver, please be quiet!"

Oliver went red. "Sorry, I'm just so terribly excited, and I can't keep my mouth shut."

Luckily, Severin Maximov now appeared in front of the pupils.

"Ten zeppelins, ten teachers," the director explained. "Ten groups of four pupils each will go on an excursion."

Maximov reached into the pocket of his brown cord jacket and pulled out a note. He unfolded it with such ceremony, he could have been about to announce the winners at the Oscars.

He pointed to the human tree. "The pupils who will be flying to the Polar Sea with Mads-Arnor Helmstad are…"

Maximov didn't get any further. Mid-sentence, something landed at his feet. A meerkat. It lay still for a moment, dazed and confused, then picked itself up again, grumbling, and tried to climb back up the nearest tree trunk.

Everyone looked up and laughed. Five metres above them, Oni was lying on a broad branch, fast asleep.

Maximov sent Helmstad to wake Oni.

"It is against the rules of the academy to spend the night in a tree!" Maximov declared, once Oni was standing before him, her knees trembling.

"But I can't sleep in closed rooms," she protested. "And in any case, I was feeling homesick, and it took me ages to fall asleep."

"Awww," whined Mary-Jay, pretending to be sympathetic, and her three friends from the clique joined in at the top of their voices.

Belle looked at Connor and rolled her eyes. But Connor didn't respond to her offer of friendship, looking off into the distance instead. What a horrible, arrogant boy!

Gradually, as the groups were announced, the pupils boarded the flying machines with their teachers. Mads-Arnor Helmstad was the first one up in the air with his team. The other two teachers Belle would have liked to fly with were already taking off too. In the end, only four pupils were left: Oni, Oliver, Belle and Connor.

"Look! All the zombies are together!" Zack bellowed down from up in the air.

Maximov summoned the four of them with a gesture of his hand.

"And now my attention turns to you," he began. Belle could already sense something wasn't right. "You won't be going on an excursion today."

"But that's not fair!" Belle blurted out.

"Not fair?" Maximov continued, calmly. "No, each of you made a negative impression in your first few hours here. And rules are important at the academy." He looked at each of them in turn.

"Oliver Snyder spent the night… *gaming.*" The director spat the word out as if it were poisonous.

"Oni Amaka left the building at night without permission, and Belle Pompadour was ten minutes late to the opening ceremony!"

Belle clenched her teeth. So her lateness had been noticed after all.

"And him?" asked Oliver, pointing to Connor.

"Connor Blaze, give me your left boot," Maximov demanded.

Connor hesitated a moment, but then succumbed and took it off.

Maximov took the boot and swivelled the sole to the side. A golden medallion fell from the secret compartment below it. It bore the image of a younger Catherine Noir.

"Attempted theft," stated Maximov tersely, pressing the boot back into Connor's hand. For the first time, Connor dropped his cool façade. He was clearly impressed.

"Well, what are you waiting for?" the academy director admonished them. "Put on some old clothes, and off you go – time for some hard labour."

Oni, Oliver and Belle watched the zeppelins longingly as, one by one, they disappeared over the horizon. Connor went back to looking as bored as ever.

Half an hour later, Maximov led the four of them up to

the castle attic with buckets, mops and cloths. The room was enormous, and packed to the rafters with peculiar objects, rolls of maps and leather-bound books.

"This is where we store the ACE's collection of artefacts that we do not – how shall I put it? – *prioritise,*" the director explained, wheezing. "No golden daggers or viable dinosaur eggs, and in fact, many items here turned out to be flops. But they too tell the story of our club."

He went over to a shelf and stroked an antique camera. "This is the camera that *nearly* took the first photograph of a yeti in 1912. Over there is a figurehead that *might* have belonged to the *Flying Dutchman,* and..." The director cleared his throat, sending a thick cloud of dust sailing across the room. "Anyway, your job is to clean everything. If you do it properly, I might think about pardoning you."

And, just as he was leaving the attic, Severin Maximov turned with a reminder. "Just dust – don't scrub!" he bellowed in a deep voice. "These are all unique pieces – irreplaceable! Don't disappoint me a second time."

With a disproportionately loud bang, he swung the door shut behind him.

"When someone says something like that in films, it's when the most expensive piece always breaks," Belle remarked, laughing. But none of the others seemed to find it funny – and none of them picked up their cleaning cloths, either.

Oni and Anubi looked longingly out of the window and down at the grounds. Connor threw himself onto a tattered sofa, and Belle studied the black sky sceptically.

"I hope the castle has a lightning conductor," she murmured. "It's getting worse and worse out there."

Oliver was the only one in good spirits. He was going from one shelf to another, his eyes sparkling. He eventually stopped in front of a cubic box with a funnel and crank handle.

"Wow!" he cried excitedly. "The thoughtophone! This telecommunications device was constructed by Hedda von Habenichts in 1841 – around thirty years before the invention of the telephone! And it's even superior to our smartphones."

Oliver adjusted the bulky device on the shelf. "Look! No cables! No antennae – all it needs to establish the connection are the caller's thoughts."

On the sofa, Connor let out an overly loud yawn. "That's complete rubbish!" he declared. "A *thoughtophone* – only grannies who believe in horoscopes would be taken in by something like that…"

Oliver gave a dismissive wave. "Quite the opposite!" he answered. "The brain – whether it belongs to a human or a leech – mostly consists of nerve cells. These transmit information with the aid of chemical messengers – or through electrical signals. Hedda von— Argh, help me, Belle." But, without waiting for her, Oliver pulled the device off the shelf himself. "Heavy as hell…" he announced.

"Hey, we're not meant to be touching anything!" cried Oni.

Oliver gave another dismissive wave. "You can't break this. Solid workmanship."

He heaved the device onto a wobbly table in the middle of the room. Then he twiddled a few knobs, pushed a lever and adjusted the angle of the funnel.

Anubi leapt towards him, full of curiosity. When Oni followed her meerkat, Belle joined them too. Oliver turned the thoughtophone on and bowed his head until his forehead was touching the copper plate.

"This transmits the signals," he explained. Then Oliver said a name. "Marike Snyder. That's my mother," he said. "I'm thinking really hard about her right now…"

"And not only now – what a mummy's boy!" Connor sneered. Belle shot him an angry look.

Oliver adjusted the knobs a little more, and suddenly a woman's voice reverberated from the funnel, speaking Dutch.

The girls stared at Oliver in fascination. Connor, however, remained sceptical.

"Pfff! That's just a radio station – does anyone here even know what your mother sounds like?"

Oliver sighed. "Okay then, let's choose someone we all know – McFinnegan?"

"Madame Noir," Connor demanded. By now, he was sitting up. It seemed he wasn't entirely unimpressed with this machine after all.

Oliver placed his head on the copper plate again.

The voice with the unmistakable accent rang out straightaway.

"Are the pupils properly occupied?" Noir was asking someone. "We don't want them suddenly turning up while we're opening the vault."

"They're cleaning the attic," Maximov growled.

"Good," said Noir. The voices sounded muffled, as if they were in an underground room. "The Fire Tiger was never in danger, Maximov."

"Tsk!" the director retorted. "You gambled recklessly with the future of the ACE!"

"I did not," Noir replied calmly. "We presented a dummy at the ceremony. The real Fire Tiger never left the safe."

Belle, Oni and Connor exchanged glances. Connor's eyebrows began to twitch.

They could hear a key being inserted into a keyhole and a heavy door creaking open.

"This here is the real Fire Ti—" Noir broke off.

Four floors above her, everyone was holding their breath.

"Where is the dagger?" Maximov cried. "And how did these bones get into the chest…?"

There was a rustling sound, then, in a trembling voice, Noir spoke. It sounded like she was reading out a message.

"Many thanks for the Fire Tiger. It can only kill one person at a time, but we will *activate* it, and then our organisation will be in possession of the most dangerous weapon in the world."

Maximov gulped. "It's BONE! They only sent the Phantom… as a decoy," he stammered. "And in the meantime they have calmly emptied out the vault—"

Suddenly, Connor well and truly lost his cool. He kicked the table leg in fury. The table tipped to one side and the thoughtophone fell to the floor and shattered into a thousand pieces. At the same time, a crack of thunder came from outside.

Belle had a feeling the world was about to dissolve under her feet.

BONE

Heavy drops of rain were drumming on the roof tiles of the castle. Lightning flashed across the pitch-black sky. Oliver, Oni, Belle and Connor were standing in a circle. But no matter how hard they stared at the fragments, the thoughtophone wasn't going to reassemble itself on its own.

"So, what should we do now?" Oni stammered. She sounded as if she was about to burst into tears.

"We get rid of the thing," suggested Belle. "It sounds like the ACE has bigger problems than an old box that's been languishing in the attic for decades anyway."

Oliver fell to his knees, ashen-faced, and rummaged around in the broken pieces.

Connor, however, was pacing up and down like a tiger in a cage.

"Maximov will notice something is missing!" he protested. "Oliver's father will be mortified by his son's behaviour, Oni's hair will go grey from the stress of being grounded, and Belle, in the eyes of all the other pupils, you'll only confirm the stereotype: nothing more than a pretty face!"

"Really?" said Belle. "What century are you from?"

Oni, Oliver and Belle stared at Connor in contempt.

"What are you looking at me like that for?" asked Connor innocently. "That's just what everyone will think. In any case, our careers at the ACE are over. Maybe they'll hang our photos up in the hall as deterrents – the fastest expulsions of all time..."

Belle gave him a hard shove on the shoulder. "All right, we get it. We've taken the definition of losers to a whole new level."

Belle's head was spinning. Ever since her dad had raced onto the castle forecourt like a madman, everything had gone downhill. Her dream of adventures had turned into a nightmare.

She'd be lucky if she was even allowed to keep scrubbing rooms full of junk! That's if the ACE didn't implode altogether. But she really wanted to stay, and something bad was happening. Belle wasn't going to give up without a fight.

"Who or what is BONE, Oliver?" she asked.

Oliver stood up and went over to a long row of dusty

books on a shelf. They all had the logo of the club embossed on the leather of their spines.

"Everything is in the ACE encyclopaedia," he informed Belle. "This here is an old edition."

Oliver ran his finger along the row until he got to B, then he sat on the floor cross-legged and opened the huge tome.

Belle and Oni knelt beside him. Connor looked over their shoulders at first, then he sat down too. Anubi squeezed through everyone to get to his mistress.

BONE

"BONE is a powerful secret alliance whose goal is nothing less than world supremacy," Oliver began reading, haltingly. "They try to accelerate their journey to this goal by means of magical artefacts. The abbreviation stands for Best Of New Explorers, because its members believe they are exactly that – the best."

Oliver turned to the next page. A pirate's face grimaced at them. Oni clutched Anubi to her. Oliver was speaking quietly now, as if the bloodthirsty scoundrel would hear him otherwise.

"This is Diablo Cortez, nicknamed 'The Bull', the arch-enemy of van Robbemond. BONE was founded a good one hundred and fifty years after the ACE, but at a push, its history could be interpreted as going back to The Bull. BONE—"

The next flash of lightning illuminated the room, and there was an almost simultaneous crack of thunder. The three bare lightbulbs on the ceiling flickered, and after that they only gave off half as much light. Oliver clung to the book. He had to take a deep breath before he was able to speak.

"BONE operates the way Cortez did. It lets other adventurers do the work then relieves them of their legendary booty. Nobody knows who belongs to BONE – it is a big secret." Oliver leafed through the book again. "Here!"

He tapped on the flag of Diablo Cortez – the skull and crossbones of a bull.

As if on cue, the next flash of lightning split the sky.

Connor leapt up and started pacing around restlessly.

"What is BONE planning?" he asked. "What do they mean by 'activating' the Fire Tiger? I thought it was already a magical weapon?"

"Indeed it is," Oliver confirmed. "But the pommel of the Fire Tiger is missing a ruby. As soon as this ruby is set back into the pommel, the dagger will become the deadliest weapon of all time. Van Robbemond took the precaution all those years ago of removing the ruby and leaving it in a temple in Indonesia in case the Fire Tiger should fall into the wrong hands. The ruby still lies there to this day. It looks like BONE wants to get its hands on it..."

"How stupid of them to divulge their plans," sniffed Belle. "Now all we need is for some ACE members to lie in wait at this temple and get the Fire Tiger back."

Oliver shook his head. "Belle, no one knows where the temple is. All we know is that it's somewhere in Indonesia."

Oni ran her fingers through Anubi's fur. She stared out of the window, lost in thought.

"Look!" she cried suddenly. Everyone rushed towards her. Belle pressed her nose up against the cold window pane. Down below, Madame Noir, Severin Maximov and two other people from the castle seemed to be in a rush. Maximov locked the castle gate and hurried after the others through the pelting rain. A zeppelin came towards them from the airport.

"That's not a Sky Explorer," murmured Oliver. "That's a Sky Divider. And it's not called that for nothing – it can fly at *twice* the speed of sound."

The zeppelin lowered itself to the ground. The four passengers were barely on board before it rose up again, shot off through the grounds, and disappeared altogether.

"Hey!" squeaked Oliver, slapping the window with the palm of his hand. "You forgot us! We're still in the castle!"

"Calm down." Connor tried to pacify him. "We won't starve. The castle's pantry is full, and we can always climb out the windows if we have to… I'm more interested in what they're up to."

Right at that moment, the funnel of the thoughtophone started to vibrate. Madame Noir's voice came through, but it was very distorted.

"We will find the temple, Maximov. There must also be some clues as to its location in the inhabitants' stories in the books of legends. First, we'll fly to…" The funnel gave a last rattle, then bounced riotously across the wooden floor and finally fell silent.

Oliver sank back down to his knees and pushed the fragments of machine together into a pile, but no further sound came out of it.

“Madame Noir is so clever – she’s bound to find it,” declared Oni from the windowsill.

Oliver pulled a face. “I doubt it. Both my grandmother and my father dedicated their lives to searching for this temple – without success.”

Connor punched a bookcase. “I just don’t believe that,” he cried. “The Fire Tiger turned van Robbemond into a completely new person, and you’re telling me he didn’t write the location of this temple down anywhere?”

Oliver bit his bottom lip. “Of course not, because that’s where the ruby is. But there’s another clue… According to the legend, a coin that is broken in half will point the way to the temple if you’re standing in van Robbemond’s chamber in Batavia. Something like the one you’re wearing on your wrist, Connor…”

Oliver’s voice faltered as he spoke these words. All eyes turned to Connor. A leather band was tied around his wrist, and hanging off it was an old gold coin that seemed to have been broken down the middle.

“If you’re making jokes about this coin, I’ll kill you!” Connor roared furiously. “It’s the only thing I have left of my mother…” But the thought of his mother clearly had a calming effect on Connor, as his tone of voice suddenly softened. "She fastened this piece of jewellery to my wrist on my third birthday and said one day I would achieve great things with it. She couldn't tell me any more, because a few days later…"

Belle placed her hand on Connor's shoulder. Connor lowered his head. His mask was beginning to crack, revealing a hint of the real Connor.

"May… may I take a look at it?" Oliver asked.

Connor wiped his eyes with the back of his hand, then nodded and held out his arm.

"I… I don't believe it…" Oliver stammered. "That's it! Van Robbemond's coin! The key to finding the temple!"

Without asking Connor for permission, he undid the knot on the bracelet and released the coin.

When he held it up towards the faint light bulb, a jagged line appeared on the floorboards. It looked like a mountain range. On one spot there was a deep notch.

"There, where the notch is pointing – that's the temple," Oliver stammered on excitedly. "You have to hold it out of the window of van Robbemond's room in Batavia and…" Oliver dropped his arm again. "Madame Noir has to have this coin, Connor. That's the only way she can beat BONE to the ruby."

Belle couldn't bring herself to join in the discussion.

Her head wouldn't stop spinning with one question in particular… *Who are you, Connor Blaze?*

Connor grabbed the coin and stuffed it in his pocket. "Small problem – she's not sitting in her office right now – she's flying to who knows where. We'll have to wait until she gets back."

"No we won't," Oni said, still perched on the windowsill. She spoke quietly, but Oliver and Connor pricked up their ears straightaway. She turned to face the others, her eyes blazing. "There's another zeppelin," she said firmly. "We'll follow Madame Noir and bring her the key to the temple!"

A Bold Plan

There was a long silence in the attic. Oni's words had triggered all kinds of ideas in everyone's heads. Suddenly, a crack of thunder shook the castle.

"So we're supposed to steal a Sky Explorer?" squeaked Oliver. "Then fly away from the academy? First the broken thoughtophone, and now… We'll be expelled!"

Connor dropped onto the sofa. "If BONE activates the Fire Tiger, it won't be long before there's no academy left to expel us from, Oliver," he said, bluntly. "We have no choice – we have to go after Noir and Maximov."

Belle looked over at Oliver. Even in the faint light, she could see his head was swimming. On one hand, he knew Connor was right. On the other, he was not one for intentionally breaking rules.

"That won't help." Oliver sighed. "Even if we manage to get the coin to Madame Noir, not a soul knows where Batavia actually is."

"Not true!" interrupted Oni. "Batavia was a small Dutch colony built on the island of Java in Indonesia. It was renamed Jakarta when Indonesia took back its independence from the Dutch colonisers. It's now the capital city!"

"Correct," confirmed Oliver, "but that was the relatively new Batavia. The old one, where van Robbemond was living when he found the Fire Tiger, was destroyed by an earthquake in 1719 – it will be impossible to find the temple. So we won't need to… *hijack* any Sky Explorer. And that's that."

"BONE found it," Belle said, "so we can find it too!"

Her eyes wandered along the encyclopaedic volumes of the history of the ACE. Were there really no clues hidden there? Suddenly, she stopped short. All the books looked the same, except one, where ACE was embossed in a different place. Belle stood up and went over to the shelf. Right then, there was a flash of lightning outside, and at the very same time, a flash of inspiration struck Belle, too: the book was upside down! And there were still embossed letters, but they were different: VOC.

Something rang a bell in Belle's mind. "VOC stands for 'Vereenigde Oostindische Compagnie' – the Dutch East India Company," she recalled. After all, she'd studied the history of the club, too. "The young van Robbemond set off towards the East in one of their ships."

Belle opened the book. Unfortunately, there was no map of Batavia with a red cross marking the temple. Instead, there were endless lists of ships' cargo. But, at the front, on the cover, was an emblem, and below it, in elaborate handwriting, an address and the date 1705.

"This book has been taken from the archive of the VOC," Belle realised in astonishment. There were butterflies in her tummy again. "Surely there must be some documents there that show which boat van Robbemond was hired on. All we need to do is check the route, and – wham! – we'll know where Batavia was!"

Oliver gave her only a brief glance, then a dismissive wave.

"It won't be 'wham!' at all," he said wearily. "I've been to the archive a hundred times with my father – or at least, it feels that way. There isn't even the slightest reference to van Robbemond anywhere. We've turned half of The Hague upside down looking for one…"

Belle was about to close the book in disappointment,

when suddenly the letters in the address written inside the book began to dance in front of her eyes.

"Oliver," she said softly. "This book here isn't from The Hague. It's from Amsterdam."

Oliver shook his head.

"That can't be true."

He pulled a magnifying glass out of his pocket and bent so far over the page that his nose almost touched the seal. Then he drizzled some liquid on the ink. It gave off a strongly acidic smell.

"It's… it's real, it's really old ink," Oliver stammered. "So, there was a secret VOC archive in Amsterdam!"

Lightning flashed four times, as if in confirmation.

Oni stood up, looking like she'd seen a ghost.

"Look, even though I don't like it," she said quietly, "there are four of us, and the sky has just sent four flashes of lightning. Our destiny is to start looking for Batavia."

Belle came and stood beside her. "I agree!"

Connor punched the air. "Yes! What about you, Oliver?"

Oliver shook his head. "I like adventures," he replied softly, "but reading about them is safer than going on them. And who's to say we'll find anything there anyway?"

Connor breathed out heavily. "You have to come – you've been outvoted."

Oliver's eyes narrowed. "Why does everyone always think they can push me around?" he cried. "I have a will of my own. And I don't want to do it!"

Belle had an idea. "You know everything about zeppelins, right?"

Oliver's eyes lit up immediately. "Yes!" he whispered. "They're the only reason why I came to the academy."

Belle's heart was beating faster. "And wouldn't you like to fly one, too?"

Oliver flushed. "I… well, I could imagine…"

Connor rolled his eyes. "Stop babbling on, man! Make a decision – yes or no?"

Oliver smiled.

"Yes!" he replied, loud and clear this time. "Yes, I'm desperate to pilot a Sky Explorer! The X9-24 model is equipped with an AI device, and if—"

"Spare us the details, Cap'n," Belle interrupted him. "Everyone – get your things together and meet at the locked gate in fifteen minutes!"

The others nodded. And then there was another flash of lightning.

Headlong Into an Adventure

Oni and Belle waited excitedly at the castle gate. Belle was still confused by the unbelievable coincidence… Oliver was telling them about a legendary coin – and Connor turned out to be wearing it on his wrist. *Was* it a coincidence? Or destiny, as Oni had claimed? Belle bit her bottom lip. This was a question which, like many things in life, didn't have an obvious answer.

"Where have the boys got to?" chuntered Belle.

Oni just shrugged her shoulders. She rattled the castle gate for the hundredth time, but it stayed locked.

Anubi was perched in her rucksack, looking around in curiosity. Suddenly, his arm shot forwards. He grabbed a moth mid-flight and, with relish, gobbled it up on the spot.

Once the bell in the castle chapel had rung five times, Oliver appeared at the top of the stairs. He dragged two suitcases, bursting at the seams, down the steps.

Connor followed shortly after. With nothing but a tiny black rucksack.

"Don't you have a bag?" Belle asked, puzzled.

Connor shook his head. "I always travel light."

He went over to the castle gate and tried the handle.

"It's locked," Belle said. "We'll have to climb over."

To her great astonishment, however, the heavy gate swung open.

"Open!" he whispered with a grin.

Oni shook her head. "Eh?" she said, mystified. "I only just tried that."

Connor shrugged his shoulders. "Then you can't have turned it properly. In all the excitement, Maximov must have turned the key in the wrong direction… Well, are you coming?"

Outside, the worst of the storm had passed. Evening had set in. The dense cloud was darkening the sky even more.

The four of them climbed up the slippery ramp to the airport. All the gangplanks were empty. Except one.

Connor leapt up onto the step in front of the door to the zeppelin. But Oliver hesitated. Was he going to back out at the last minute?

"This zeppelin was supposed to be for our group anyway," Belle tried again to persuade Oliver. "We're doing the right thing. Noir needs the coin."

Oliver gulped. Finally, he nodded and took the hand Connor was holding out towards him. The door behind Connor was now open.

"Not locked either," remarked Connor, when he noticed Belle's puzzled look. "The ACE members appear to have a problem with keys."

Belle and Oni followed the two boys on board.

Inside, it smelled of old wood and pipe tobacco. Connor turned on a tiny torch.

The airship consisted of a large, long room, which probably served as a classroom. Maps and books were lying around, and some were stored on a narrow shelf. Old writing tools, a pair of compasses and a thick notebook with symbols scribbled on it were spread across the table. The walls had reddish wood panelling, and three doors led off to other rooms.

"Bedrooms," Oni surmised. "Which can be closed up, like our rooms in the castle," she added, with a shudder.

Anubi browsed around this unfamiliar environment, wide-eyed. Then he scurried outside again before coming back to snuffle at the middle of the three bedroom doors. When he started scratching at it, Oni whistled for him to come to her.

"There aren't any beetles in there, Anubi," she said gently.

Belle went over to the cockpit at the front of the zeppelin. Oliver had taken his place in the pilot's seat and was flipping a few switches. Somewhere above them, they heard the hum of a motor starting up.

"Okay, the strato-compensator is running, so we won't drop down straightaway," Oliver announced, concentrating on the dashboard. "Connor, cast off!"

Connor leaned outside and pulled up the rope.

The zeppelin immediately sank.

Anubi clung to Oni's leg.

"Wooaah…!" Oliver exclaimed. "Stay with me, now…!"

He tapped around on the floor with his foot until he found what he was looking for. Somehow, he got the airship to gradually pull up again.

"Phew!" Oliver sighed in relief. "That was close…"

Right at that moment, the lights went on across the whole room. Above Oliver, a device was released from the ceiling. Oliver brought his hands up to protect his head. But the device curved around him, almost as if it were weightless, then hung in the air right in front of his eyes.

Carefully, Oliver let his hands drop. The device was like a games console with little lamps of every colour flashing on the front. Two of them were sending out green

waves – Oliver's face was being scanned.

"You are not Harold!" an artificial voice declared. "Harold has a beard."

"Are you… the AI device?" Oliver asked. By now, Connor was in the cockpit, too. The zeppelin was overbalancing in a forward direction, its nose pointing down into the grounds.

"I am TICI – Thing I Cannot Improve," replied the box. "My task is to bring the Sky Explorer X9-24 safely to its destination. But perhaps I had better inform Harold that you—"

"No, no, not necessary," Belle interrupted the machine. "We want to go to Amsterdam. Can you manage that?"

All of TICI's lights came on. "Amsterdam, Netherlands, European mainland. Estimated arrival in sixteen minutes and twenty-one seconds. Please enter the security code and confirm."

Belle looked over at the others. Oliver shrugged his shoulders and Oni sighed.

"Let me have a go," said Connor, jostling Oliver out of the seat. "I know a bit about security systems."

Connor fished out a calculator of some sort from his tiny rucksack, attached it to the dashboard and tapped around on the keys. Green numbers ran across a screen.

Finally, something beeped.

"Code correct. Permission to take off granted," TICI reverberated, adding in astonishment, "by the way, I have no idea how you did that!"

Slowly, the airship pushed off from the port. Half a mile from the castle, TICI switched to full boost, and the Sky Explorer raced off at supersonic speed.

Connor leapt up from the seat, thrusting his arms in the air. Oliver flung his arms around Connor's neck, and Oni and Belle joined in. Anubi climbed on top of them all, squealing in excitement.

"We did it! We did it!" all four of them cheered.

Then, the middle of the three doors flew open. Harold Godric McFinnegan entered the room wearing an old-fashioned nightshirt and cap. "What's going on here?" he snarled. It didn't sound like his four pupils were going to get much further on their journey.

McFinnegan stopped the zeppelin over the English Channel. They could hear seagulls screeching outside the window. Anubi was crouching on the window ledge, trying to spot them in the darkness. Everyone else was sitting silently around the map table. Connor's half coin lay in front of them.

McFinnegan had put on his tweed suit and then listened to their story in silence.

"Your motives were admirable," he began, "Catherine must have the coin – and the information about Batavia's location. But you didn't need to fly off into the unknown. All the zeppelins are connected to one another through a secret radio frequency, which means I'll be able to fetch Noir back and we can all return to the castle."

He went into the cockpit and sat down.

"TICI, establish radio contact with the president's Sky Divider," he commanded.

TICI flew over to him. "Negative," she replied. "The president has blocked all frequencies. This is a Code Red."

"Highest level of alert, okay, okay…" muttered McFinnegan. "In that case, locate her and I'll just have to fly after her."

"Double negative," the AI device reverberated. "The location function has also been deactivated. No wonder, given the current situation. Analysis of all available information suggests it is not unlikely that there is a mole in the ACE who is passing on information to BONE."

McFinnegan snorted. "Well then, we must return to Deep Fog Castle."

Oliver lowered his head. Connor's lips were trembling.

“I’m responsible for these four pupils,” McFinnegan continued. “I’m sure Noir will get in contact with—”

“Harold, what are you doing?” TICI interrupted him. “The chances of recapturing the dagger increase by a measly 9.6 per cent if the esteemed president gets this coin in three days. However, they increase by 78.5 per cent if she gets this signpost to the temple and more precise information on the location of Batavia within the next twelve hours. And just as an aside – the chances of your pupils becoming popular among their peers increase by 84 per cent if you fly to Amsterdam.”

McFinnegan muttered incomprehensibly to himself, then spun the steering wheel round again. “Okay, fine. But only to Amsterdam!” he muttered through his beard. “BONE seems to already have that precise information and is now on the other side of the world. So we need to be sure…”

None of the pupils dared cheer, but everyone secretly punched the air.

"We must go to this address," said Belle, holding the book from the archive open towards TICI. The AI device extended a tube that looked like a reading lamp. There was a kind of eye on the end of it.

"Affirmative," replied TICI. "The name of the street was changed in 1880, but the building you are looking for still exists. A warehouse in the port of Amsterdam."

The zeppelin raced off again straightaway.

Belle was thrilled. "Yes, that must be it. Thank you, TICI."

"You're welcome, person-who-is-not-Harold," replied TICI.

Belle smiled. "I'm Belle," she introduced herself. "And the other people who are not Harold are called Oni, Oliver and Connor, and the little fellow with fur is Anubi."

"Pleased to meet you all," replied TICI. "I am now activating camouflage mode. We have arrived. Rope ladder will be released in ten seconds," TICI announced.

"But that's pointless, TICI," McFinnegan grumbled. "It's after 9 p.m. – every archive in the world will be closed by now."

Nonetheless, Connor opened the zeppelin's door. Without the slightest hesitation, he climbed down to the bottom rung of the ladder and glided on it to the ground.

"That's all the better," he called out to the others. "Seeing as I've no intention of asking for permission to enter!"

After a moment of wavering, Oni grabbed her meerkat, placed him on her shoulder, and followed Connor down. Oliver didn't look too keen to step out onto a rope ladder fifty metres above the ground. But it seemed he was even less enthusiastic about staying up there on his own with his teacher, for he too overcame his fear.

Belle looked at McFinnegan. "And you?"

"You've got me into a fine mess here, TICI!" The Scotsman sighed, clinging tightly to the top rung of the ladder. But he still looked a little like he was enjoying himself.

"Thanks, TICI!" whispered Belle, following her teacher down.

A moment or two later, the five of them were standing in the gravelled grounds of a derelict brick warehouse. There was a narrow entrance door and a larger gate at the end of the warehouse. A yardstick was marked with lines and dates, showing which years there had been flooding.

"No, we've gone wrong somewhere," whispered Oliver. He pointed to the sign under the roof, which said 'Tea and Spices, Import/Export' in faded red letters.

Connor laughed. "So what kind of sign were you expecting, Einstein?" he asked. "'Unknown VOC archive – top secret?'"

Oni closed her eyes for a moment and sniffed the air. "I can't smell anything, and I'm good at identifying herbs and plants."

Belle noticed something, too. "The last floods were in 2015, 2016 and 2019 – a warehouse that floods regularly is hardly a good place to store tea."

McFinnegan nodded. "The name seems to be a cover for something," he muttered.

Oliver rattled the handle. "Either way, we can't get in," he declared. "It's not exactly a budget lock. Not even the Phantom could manage this one."

"Tsk!" said Connor. "What do you know about the Phantom, anyway?"

Oliver put his hands on his hips. "Quite a lot," he retaliated. "After all, I touched them yesterday. Well, nearly..."

Connor snorted. Now he was even angrier. "Nearly touched – well, bravo. That must make you a real Phantom expert!"

"Is now *really* the time to start arguing about people who aren't even here?" Belle intervened. "I thought we were trying to get into the warehouse?"

"But it's impossible," Oliver squeaked. "Because not even the Phantom, if they were here—"

"Yes, they could!" cried Connor. "The Phantom could sure as hell get in here!" Connor pulled something that was flashing out of his rucksack, and rammed it into the lock. "You'll see."

Not Like a Needle in a Haystack

"You're the Phantom?" Oni, Belle and Oliver cried out at the same time.

Connor replied in his own way: he opened the sliding gate.

"I don't believe it!" whispered Oliver. "We have a wanted criminal in our midst."

Belle shook her head, smiling. "That's why you weren't at the ceremony that evening. And that's why you don't have any luggage." She was working it all out as she spoke. "You didn't know you'd be needing any."

"I made a deal with your president," Connor revealed. "She thought the ACE could do with a guy like me. And I thought it would be fun to check out your pad. Better than prison, eh?"

Oni grimaced. "Sounds like the beginning of a beautiful friendship," she said vitriolically. "I bet you'll be off at the first opportunity, anyway."

“Noir and Maximov know my identity,” retorted Connor. “And you too, now. The Phantom can’t come back – he’s dead. But Connor Blaze is alive, and he’d damn well like to get into this warehouse.”

Harold Godric McFinnegan clearly hadn’t been briefed by the director. He was staring at Connor with a puzzled look on his face.

Oliver shook his head. “You’re… you’re a thief. Why should we trust you?”

Belle nodded.

Connor swept his arm towards the door, inviting them through. “Because I’m the guy who opens doors for you!”

McFinnegan cleared his throat. “Well, I’m more than a little surprised by this information, too. But if Catherine trusts him, we should do the same.”

Connor looked each of them straight in the eye, one after the other. “Whether you trust me is up to you. But you can be sure of one thing: I’ll do anything to get the Fire Tiger back from BONE!”

“You won’t get that far, young Connor,” McFinnegan countered. “I only allowed you this one stop! Whether you find anything or not – we’re flying back to the academy early tomorrow!”

Without saying anything in response, Connor disappeared into the dark warehouse.

Belle had a thousand questions she was burning to ask. But she knew Connor would only give her snarky answers now. So she did what they had come to do.

“Off you go,” she commanded, shoving Oliver and Oni through the gate. “Let’s give him a chance.”

McFinnegan stayed standing in the gravelled area. “I’ll keep watch,” he growled, shaking his head. “What on earth have I got myself into…?”

Belle followed the others. It was pitch-black in the warehouse. The few windows were covered in a thick layer of dust. No light was penetrating through from the street lamps. Suddenly, Connor was standing in front of her.

“Here!” he said, pressing a second torch into Belle’s hand. “I’ve no idea what we’re looking for, but you had the right instinct when we were up there in the attic.”

Belle bit her bottom lip. Coming from Connor, that was almost praise. She looked at him, but his dark eyes were inscrutable. Whatever was going on in Connor’s head, he’d learnt to conceal it.

Belle shone the torch around in a circle. Endless rows of shelves ran side by side down the clinically clean room. The lowest shelves were all empty, surely because of the flooding. But from about one metre off of the floor, right up to the ceiling were files upon files upon files. There must have been millions of documents. It didn't look anything like a secret archive. More like a load of tedium and administration.

"We're bound to find the clue we're looking for among all these records," said Belle, without sounding at all convinced. "You and Connor start on the right-hand side, Oni. Oliver and I will take the shelves on the left."

It didn't take long for Belle to start to regret this pairing. Once again, Oliver couldn't keep his mouth shut.

"The Dutch East India Company has existed since 1602," he trotted out. "Over four hundred years!"

Belle nodded. And the majority of their cargo papers, rental contracts and other paperwork was stored in this warehouse, away from the publicly accessible archive. At least the dates were on the shelf racks – that made things easier. The four of them paced quickly backwards through the centuries.

"The year of van Robbemond's birth has been officially declared as 1677," Oliver went on. "At the age of 14, he was hired by the Dutch East India Company, the VOC – which means we need to look out for documents from 1691 to around 1710."

"Zut alors!" Belle cursed. The dating on the shelves stopped at 1750.

“Why isn’t there a flashing arrow saying ‘this way to documents for the Fire Tiger’?” said Connor.

Oliver pulled a face. “Because then… Ah, that wasn’t a real question, was it?”

Belle shook her head. “It’s like looking for a needle in a haystack,” she continued.

“Actually, it’s not. Not really,” Oliver said. “We simply have to keep an eye out for what we’re not looking for!”

“What?” Belle said.

“Is there anything here that is out of place?” Oliver replied.

Connor nodded in silence. Oliver’s tactic seemed to make sense to him.

“I have noticed something, actually,” he whispered. “Come with me!”

The light from the two torches swept back to the middle of the room. Connor stopped in front of a round metal plate. Beside it, there were fresh scratches in the wooden floor.

“There you go, Oliver,” he said. Despite the darkness, Belle knew Connor was grinning.

“Think of the marks on the yardstick outside,” he reminded the others. “The place is constantly flooding. Everything else made of metal in here has gone completely rusty. But the screws on this lid look like new."

Belle was astonished. "I would never have noticed that," she admitted. "But how does it help us?"

Connor swept his torch around the room. "All this junk in here is just a distraction – a haystack, as Belle rightly described it. The actual treasure of this secret archive is… here!"

As Connor was giving his little lecture to the others, he managed to loosen the five finger-thick screws in the round metal plate without them noticing. Now he pushed the plate to the side and shone his torch into the circular hole that lay beneath. A good twenty metres down, it illuminated a wooden plank with a name engraved on it, and beside that a sailor's chest and all kinds of ships' paraphernalia.

"Brilliant, Connor!" exclaimed Belle. "So what are we waiting for? Maybe it leads to the museum!"

Oliver pulled a face. "And what if somebody comes?" Oliver mumbled. "Then we'll be caught."

"Well, I'm going down!" Oni whispered. "The sooner I'm back outside, the better."

Step by step, Oni climbed down the iron ladder on the wall, into the depths of the shaft. Belle held the torch between her teeth and followed her. The shaft was narrow.

It smelled musty, and the icy cold came racing up towards her. To make things worse, Oliver stood on her finger.

But when Belle saw what was at the bottom, she forgot all about that. The low-ceilinged room was a real treasure chamber. Down here, there were hundreds of things that any maritime museum would have paid huge sums of money for: nautical charts inscribed on leather, ships' parts, cannonballs, and a huge brass compass.

"Why are they hiding all this?" asked Oni.

Connor shrugged. "I'm pretty sure these are all things

that don't come up in the official history of the company – a few employees' dodgy deals from times gone by…"

Belle picked up a sword and held the tip under Connor's chin. "Phantom, confess to your crimes!" she demanded, laughing.

Connor shoved the weapon out of the way with his arm.

"Stop messing around," he barked at Belle. "BONE was here, and not long ago either. Every second we fritter away—"

"Quiet!" hissed Belle suddenly.

Everyone immediately held their breath. They could hear something moving about in the warehouse above. Connor and Belle turned off their torches. Shortly after that, a face appeared above their heads.

"Anubi!" cried Oni, breathing a sigh of relief. "In all the excitement, I completely forgot about you!"

Belle relaxed a little. Connor going on about BONE had made her really nervous.

"We still need to hurry," Connor insisted. He tied his torch to the ceiling with a piece of wire so that everyone had light. There could be a clue to Batavia hiding absolutely anywhere down here. Let's find it!"

So the four of them set about closely examining every object in the underground hidey-hole.

"I-I don't believe it," Oliver suddenly stammered,

pulling a huge tome out of the sailor's chest. "Van Robbemond's logbook – the first part, which everyone thought was missing! If my father only knew!"

Everyone raced over to him. Oliver sat on the sailor's chest and opened the book, his fingers trembling. Dust rose up towards him. Belle shone her torch over his shoulder.

The pages of the logbook were crammed with writing. But it was all very elaborate, and in any case, it was in another language.

"Zut alors!" she hissed. "We didn't think of that. No one can read it."

Oliver pushed his glasses back up his nose with his middle finger. "I can – it's Dutch. He does use lots of words that aren't in common use any more, but with a bit of time, I could probably translate it all."

"Get going, then," Belle urged. "What does it say?"

Oliver let out a sigh. "There are easily two hundred pages here – there's no way I'm reading all that out to you now. Let's take it with us."

Connor gave a dismissive wave. "I bet there aren't even any secrets in it. Otherwise the people from BONE wouldn't have left it here. Damn it!"

Exasperated, he tried to snatch the logbook out of Oliver's hands. But Oliver didn't let go. He clutched his treasure tightly with both hands. Connor pulled… Oliver pulled, tearing apart the brittle leather on the spine in the process. Something slipped out.

All four of them stared, spellbound, at the parchment that was now sailing down to the ground from its hiding place. It was the hand-drawn site plan of a town. Above it was a word: Batavia!

A Bucket Full of Blood

Alfred P. Hades was sitting at his desk in New York, looking at his laptop. Four children ran across the screen. They stopped by McFinnegan, held a book and a map under his nose, then disappeared from the warehouse grounds. None of them had noticed the camera, which was transmitting images from its position above the gate.

"Stupid old fool," muttered Alfred P. Hades, closing his laptop in satisfaction. It was dark at BONE headquarters, on the ninety-nineth floor of his office block. Pitch-black. All the windows were bricked up.

The boss of BONE was allergic to light. His skin was paler than snow. That's why he was called the White Shadow. Like a shadow, he could stick close to his adversaries.

Although he was the brains behind all of BONE's operations, the White Shadow never got his own hands dirty. He preferred to deploy the members of BONE to do the work – they always followed his orders unconditionally. At the moment, Alexander Malus was the most useful to him. That's why he was now dialling his number.

*

The zeppelin was already on its fifteenth lap of Amsterdam as the sun came up over the horizon.

Harold Godric McFinnegan was pacing up and down the classroom like a caged tiger.

“We must fly back!” he asserted. “Anything else is too dangerous!”

But as he spoke, he doubled over with what looked to Belle like stomach pains.

“Harold! What are you talking about?” TICI admonished him. “You have to go to Java! Catherine Noir needs the amulet, and she will be there. The chances of getting the coin to her increase by 100 per cent if you go.”

“Mrrrggh,” said McFinnegan. He let out a deep sigh, then adjusted his tie and pulled himself together.

“TICI, destination: coast of Java, location of the old Batavia,” McFinnegan commanded, as if he’d never even considered going back to the castle.

The four pupils started cheering.

“We’re only going to check the position of the old Batavia,” McFinnegan reminded them. “Then we’ll hand over the map and coin to Catherine – Madame Noir. If her Sky Divider really is over there, we can locate it from a short distance away, even with conventional radar.”

Connor nodded, but Belle could see in his eyes that he

wasn't going to let anyone stop him getting the Fire Tiger back.

Once TICI had switched to supersonic mode, the Scotsman cleared the map table. Their classroom flew off towards the East. Now they had plenty of time to study the text on the back of the map more closely. Anubi found himself a quiet corner among the book shelves and curled up in a ball. He'd clearly had enough excitement for one day.

Oliver sat down and placed Connor's lucky charm on the map. "So, we know where the old Batavia was," he recapped, "but if we want to find the temple, we need to know exactly where van Robbemond lived when he wasn't on his ship. The coin can only point us in the direction of the temple if we are standing in his chamber and holding it out of the window."

Belle and Oni looked over his shoulder. The strip of coastline had been traced in precise detail – even a few palm trees had been drawn on it. And a wind rose showing the points of the compass had been drawn in the top-left corner. In the top-right corner there was a drawing of an Indonesian woman. Judging by her magnificent headdress, she was probably a princess or a priestess.

Oliver pushed the sawn-off coin across the map. But

nowhere did the lines drawn on the map align with the slits in the coin.

"Shame," Oliver murmured. "I thought maybe…"

"You'll find it," Belle encouraged him, turning the map around. Awestruck, she ran her fingers over the elaborate letters on the page. Suddenly, she saw van Robbemond before her, sitting in the cabin of his ship, writing these very words on the paper with a quill pen.

"It's a letter," Oliver declared once he'd deciphered the first few words. "Eleven-Fingered Louie, my good friend!" he read haltingly. But all Belle could hear was the pirate's voice speaking. "Since the Fire Tiger has been in my possession, my whole life has changed. Henceforth, instead of plundering, I will seek magical artefacts and protect them from devious people. I have decided to found a club of adventurers, and I want you to be at my side – you know the Indonesian waters like no other. I have also persuaded Princess Li and Samson Mbeke to join me. We are meeting on the first Sunday of April in my chamber in Emmer Bloed to hold our first conference. The map will show you the way. And bring your wanderboots with you."

Oni nudged Oliver. "Wanderboots? Does he mean something like hiking boots? Sounds like a strange thing for a pirate to wear. Maybe it's a hidden clue? The temple must be at the top of a mountain and hard to reach. Read on!"

Oliver shook his head. "This is where the letter ends, but we've got enough clues. Emmer Bloed is a reference to a legendary tavern in Batavia. It translates as Bucket Full of Blood."

"Great marketing," scoffed Belle. "Makes you want to take a seat and order an iced tea…"

Connor laughed. "I've got a feeling the guests in the pirate tavern probably had different drinks of choice to you."

McFinnegan cleared his throat impatiently. "TICI, how much further is it now?"

"Almost exactly five metres, Harold," TICI replied. "We've been hovering over the position for ninety-two seconds."

Oni, Connor, Oliver and Belle dashed to the window, but they couldn't see any house ruins or shipwrecks full of seashells beneath them. There was nothing but rocks, mangrove trees and ocean, as far as the eye could see.

"Is this the right place, TICI?" Belle asked.

"Of course!" the AI device snapped. "Admittedly, earthquakes like that have a habit of reshaping the landscape somewhat. Should I turn back?"

"No way!" interrupted Connor. "We're going down

there. TICI, switch to camouflage mode and release the rope ladder!"

McFinnegan cleared his throat again. "I'm sure you'll be a good zeppelin pilot one day, young Connor," he growled. "But right now, I'm still giving the orders."

"TICI, take us down," said McFinnegan. "Camouflage on, and release rope ladder!"

Connor couldn't suppress a grin. "Couldn't have put it better myself, Mr McFinnegan!"

Once they touched down, no one was laughing any more. How had TICI put it? *Earthquakes have a habit of reshaping the landscape somewhat* – that was rather an understatement. Some of the rocks were as big as houses; even the smallest were the size of cars. The mountain range that appeared to be illustrated on Connor's coin couldn't possibly exist any more. And there wasn't the slightest trace of a town.

"No Batavia, no Bucket Full of Blood," declared Connor, spitting frustratedly into the sea.

"I don't believe it!" Belle retorted. "Is that how quickly the legendary Phantom gives up? If old Batavia was so easy to find, someone would surely have found it before us, don't you think? Where's your fighting spirit?"

Connor didn't reply. He just squatted on one of the thousands of rocks.

McFinnegan was wiping fat beads of sweat off his brow with the back of his hand. "I'm definitely more suited to Scottish weather," he grumbled.

Oliver held Connor's coin in front of his eye and turned around in a circle.

"Nothing," he squeaked in disappointment. "There's not even the slightest correlation between the mountain ridges and the zigzags on the coin."

"We'd need someone who could look under the rocks," Oni suggested tentatively. "Hey, look over there!" Beaming with delight, she pointed to the mangroves along the coast. Their shady treetops were covered in furry animals.

"Oni!" Belle cried angrily. "We're trying to make some progress here, and all you're doing is staring at squirrels! Can't you forget your love of animals even for a minute?"

"Calm down – I want to make progress, too," Oni snapped back, "but considering that seems to be impossible for us humans, we probably need some help. From the fruit bats, for example." Without listening to the apology Belle was giving, Oni fished an amulet out from beneath her top and stroked it with her fingers. It immediately began to glow.

"What is that?" Belle asked.

"My great-grandmother gave me it," Oni revealed.

"It contains the poison fang and scales of a black mamba. With the aid of this, well, I can talk to animals."

"Oh, wow!" said Belle, stunned. "I've always wanted to be able to do that. And your grandma taught you?"

"My *great*-grandma," Oni corrected her. "She is the queen of a widespread tribe of shamans and magi in Ethiopia. I learnt everything about animals and plants from her. But my mum moved to Germany because of Dad's job, so now I'm always travelling back and forth between Africa and Europe."

Then Oni turned around and shouted out some incomprehensible words in the direction of the mangroves. A fruit bat came fluttering over and landed clumsily on the rocks.

"Hello, sweetie!" Oni greeted it.

Harold McFinnegan smiled. It looked like this wasn't the first time he'd seen Oni's ability.

"You have to help me," Oni went on. "Go and see if there are any houses hidden among the rocks, like the ones humans live in!"

The fruit bat nodded as if it had understood, shrieking excitedly in the process.

In an instant, thousands and thousands of bats rose out of the tops of the mangroves. They flew off down the coastline like a black storm cloud. They fluttered into every crevice between the rocks, disappeared for a long time, and reappeared in all kinds of different places.

As the swarm dispersed, a single fruit bat was left circling around, about one hundred metres away. It reported back to Oni in little shrieks.

"Thank you!" Oni called to it. "We're coming!"

Belle could feel her mouth had dropped open again. Fortunately, no one had looked over at her in the past few minutes.

"Did the flying ferrets really understand you?" she asked, grinning.

Oni looked at her, appalled, then noticed Belle was giggling.

"Yes, and they're actually really happy you recognised them as mammals," Oni joked back.

She grabbed Anubi and clambered from one rock to another.

Connor hopped along behind her. Oliver followed them cautiously on all fours.

McFinnegan just kept shaking his head happily. "Well, if old Batavia really is there, then… then…"

He broke off, as if one word too many might puncture the dream.

Belle helped him over the slippery rocks, but just as they reached Oni, Oliver and Connor, the teacher lost his footing. His right leg disappeared, up to his knee, down a crevice.

Connor and Oliver pulled him carefully back out again – and broke into a cheer.

"There's a house down there!" cried Connor, high-fiving Oliver. "We've found old Batavia!"

Through the boulders, Belle could see several beams and the rest of a roof. Behind this, in the dim light, she could make out an entire street of houses. It was full of rocks, shells and aquatic plants, but had otherwise survived the centuries very well.

"There's actually an entrance here!" Now Belle was cheering, too. "We just have to move a few rocks away, then we can stroll through the pirate town just like van Robbemond!"

Suddenly, Belle felt McFinnegan's fingers digging into her shoulder.

"What…?" she started to ask, but then she saw it, too.

Two huge pitch-black horses were trotting across the sky towards the coast. Only as they came closer did Belle realise they were made of metal.

"Alex Malus," McFinnegan stammered. "I should have known he'd be involved…"

Captured

Oni, Connor and Belle sat with grazed fingers and knees on the spongy floorboards of a house that no one had entered for more than three hundred years. The rope that had been used to tie them to the thick supporting beams was cutting into their wrists. Around them, almost all the furniture and other objects had been washed away by the sea. Despite the rocks resting on top of the house, however, the walls had stood astonishingly firm.

Belle was more exhausted than she'd ever been in her life. With all the hard work she'd just done, sure, but mainly with rage. They'd been doing heavy lifting for the men from BONE for hours. They'd lugged stones around, shovelled sand and rolled rocks to the side before they could finally climb

down into Batavia. And by way of thanks, these guys had tied them up in here.

Oni was sobbing. The men had captured little Anubi and tied a tether around his neck. This was obviously breaking her heart.

"We didn't even have to get our own hands dirty," said the younger of the two men, Alex Malus, with a broad grin. "Should we leave the rest to the high tide, or do you want to deal with them, Tyron?"

Alex Malus glanced over at his sidekick, who answered to the blood-curdling name of Tyron the Tyrant. He was short, his right eye was constantly blinking, and he had a long scar running from his ear to his chin. His head was covered in stubbly hairs, which looked as if he shaved once a week with a blunt and rusty knife. His hands were huge, and as strong as screw clamps; each of the four pupils had felt their force already. The scumbag was currently manhandling a floundering Oliver.

"Hold nice and still, little lad," he threatened. "A bone like that can break very quickly." Oliver immediately stopped thrashing about.

It was only by chance that Oliver, and not Connor, had ended up in this predicament. When the criminals had overpowered them, Oliver was still carrying Connor's coin. Somehow, the men knew the coin was with them, and what it could do.

"Good boy!" Tyron praised Oliver. Then he looked down at Belle, Oni and Connor. "No, no need to deal with them now," he said in answer to Malus's question. "Once we've activated the Fire Tiger, I'll be sending enough people to hell. The sea will take what it wants anyway…"

He let out a ghastly laugh, like a villain in a gangster film – where he would no doubt have been very much at home.

McFinnegan was tied to an old chair.

"How could you sink so low, Malus?" he asked his former pupil, the disdain clear in his voice.

Malus wheeled round. "That shouldn't surprise you in the least, McFinnegan!" he growled back furiously. "After all, you're the one who wrote on my expulsion papers: 'Alex does not have any respect for rules'."

McFinnegan yanked at his bonds. "Because you conducted experiments like Dr Frankenstein, implanting beating hearts into animals made of metal. I couldn't – and didn't wish to – tolerate such barbarism."

Alex Malus went right up close to him.

"But I was successful!" he boasted. "As you just saw with your own eyes. My father would have been proud of me – if you lot hadn't killed him!" Malus snorted in fury.

"Now I'm going to get some delayed satisfaction," he said with a grin. "You're going to show us the way to van Robbemond's chamber, map-master. And then the little laddie with the parting and the sleeveless jumper will let his coin do the talking. The Fire Tiger wants its rightful power back. Anyone who holds the dagger in their hands can feel it!" Alex Malus untied McFinnegan, then grabbed him by the collar and dragged him from the chair. "Bid goodbye to your protégés – or rather, bid them a good death. You've failed, old man, as you have so many times before!"

Malus hustled the teacher outside through a low doorway. Tyron got Oliver in a headlock and set off to follow them, but Oliver fought back.

"Let me at least say goodbye to Connor," he wailed. "He shares a room with me, and he's the best friend I ever had!"

Tyron rolled his eyes. "No tricks, okay? I wouldn't want to end up lugging you around because I'd had to break your legs!"

Oliver fell on his knees before Connor and hugged him firmly, whispering, "Look for Emmer Bloed. McFinnegan and I will lead them to the other end of the town. We'll try and shake them off, and then we'll come back to you – Batavia was enormous, so it will a take a long—"

"Let's go!" urged Tyron. "We haven't got all day. You can cry about your friends on the way!"

Belle jerked her rope. "You're forgetting a minor detail," she said. But the thug had already grabbed Oliver and was shoving him outside.

"Why didn't you do anything?" Belle shouted at Connor. "You've got all those pickpocketing tricks up your sleeve – couldn't you have got the rope off somehow?"

Connor tugged at his fetters for the hundredth time, but they still weren't getting any looser.

"While a freaky Frankenstein is standing in front of me with the Fire Tiger in his hand?" Connor shot back harshly. "That's a good idea, Belle. Shame I didn't come up with it myself. But you, of course, could have applied the survival strategy you used in the Sahara when you—"

"Stop!" That was the last straw for Oni. "If you don't stop arguing right away, I'll scream! The water is rising, in case you hadn't noticed. And I can hold my breath for quite a long time, but not for eight hours until the tide goes out again. So unless you have any idea how to get out of here alive, please shut up. Thank you!"

Belle realised she was being childish. It really wasn't the right time to be arguing. The water was rising relentlessly. She could feel her T-shirt getting wetter and wetter with each wave. They had, at the most, thirty minutes before they'd be facing a wretched, watery death.

"Can't Anubi bite through the rope?" she suggested in desperation.

Oni shook her head.

"It's made of plastic – he won't manage it," she muttered.

Anubi climbed up the post as far as the rope would allow. Oni's eyes followed him sadly. Suddenly, the meerkat began ranting and raving like a hungry chimpanzee, pointing excitedly at the water.

The head of an otter popped up. Its black saucer eyes studied the group, full of curiosity. When it climbed onto a beam, Oni held her breath.

The otter's fur had a striking pattern on the chest – a skull and crossbones…

"It's Jopie…!" Oni cried in amazement.

Belle was bewildered, too. Everyone had heard of the otter, of course – Jopie had been van Robbemond's animal sidekick. But that was a few hundred years ago.

Now a second otter was winding its way towards them, and a third, and a fourth. All of them were emblazoned with a skull and crossbones.

"They must be Jopie's descendants!" Belle realised.

"I hope they have inherited Jopie's intelligence as well as his fur," Connor muttered. "We haven't got much time left."

Oni snorted indignantly. "Anubi's already come up with a plan," she explained.

Belle saw the amulet around Oni's neck light up. Oni was talking to the otters in an incomprehensible language. The otters were sitting quietly on a beam, listening like attentive school pupils. Eventually, the first otter nodded, slid into the water and paddled towards Oni. It set to work with its teeth, at which point the others swam over to Belle and Connor. Within a few moments, all three were free. Anubi whooped for joy, making strange noises that Oni must have understood, for she hugged her beloved pet tightly.

"That's the second time you've saved us with your magic, Oni," Belle complimented her, rubbing her painful wrists. "Never again will I think of animals as primitive beings, I promise you that." She stroked her liberator's slick fur. "Thank you, Jopie Two," she said. "Connor's hunch was right. You're as clever as your your great-great-great – however many greats – grandad."

"Come on," Connor chimed in. "Who knows how long Oliver and McFinnegan can keep those two busy!"

With adrenalin running through every vein, Oni, Connor and Belle stepped through the door the gangsters had used ten minutes earlier.

Above them was the crevice they had climbed through to get down to old Batavia. A dark alleyway lay ahead of them, waist-high with water. And with each wave, the water continued to rise. Houses in various conditions were crammed together to the left and right. Some of them had little more than the supporting beams left; others looked as if their inhabitants had just popped out on an errand. It wasn't hard to imagine drunken pirates singing as they staggered from one tavern to the next along this street.

"We have no choice – we have to go down here!" Connor rasped, wading into the alleyway.

Belle and Oni, with Anubi on her shoulder, followed him. Their progress was slow through the high water. Belle's legs kept knocking against hard objects. She didn't dare imagine what kind of things might be bobbing around beneath the surface.

Suddenly, Oni shrieked. A pallid skeletal hand was looming up from the water. The arm was moving with the waves – it looked like a cursed creature was beckoning the three of them into hell.

"He's dead," Connor said tersely. "He can't hurt you. I'm more afraid of the living."

"Stop trying to play it cool!" Belle grumbled at him. "I mean, have you ever seen a corpse?"

Connor nodded. "More than once," he replied calmly. "I was always running away from the orphanage. The best hiding place was the cemetery. Sometimes I lived there for weeks before they captured me again."

Belle didn't say any more. Connor's life had been entirely different to hers.

They waded on in silence. Luckily, the alleyway led up to higher ground in old Batavia, where there were only puddles of water. Connor, Belle and Oni looked through every window into the houses. Skulls stared back at them through hollow eyes.

Each time, Oni turned away immediately, but Belle tried to stay calm. The few rays of sunlight coming through the crevices between the rocks only made everything even more ghostly. There was no trace of McFinnegan or Oliver, and they couldn't find any sign of van Robbemond's residence, either.

Suddenly, though, Connor stopped in front of a single-storey house. He put his finger on his lips and pointed to the sign over the door. "Emmer Bloed" was scorched deep into the wood.

"This is where van Robbemond was planning to meet Eleven-Fingered Louie and the other two in order to set up the ACE," Connor reminded them. "This was his chamber."

Belle took a deep breath. "Okay," she whispered, "I'll go first."

Eleven-Fingered Louie

Alfred P. Hades had received the report from Malus in New York and, in return, had told him about the coin that one of the boys had in his possession. About THE coin.

Alexander was the son of the twenty-first president of the ACE, Johan Malus. The old man was accused of misconduct, but before he could be brought to justice, he disappeared without trace on a dubious expedition. Alex, however, was convinced the ACE had done away with him.

Only with his help and old Malus's keys had he been able to get the Fire Tiger out of the vault. But now the White Shadow was worried that Malus might lose his temper and mess everything up.

So he left his office, hurtled 103 storeys down in the lift, and came out again ten metres below ground. Here, he switched on his mechanical horses, climbed into his coach, and moments later was galloping across the evening sky from New York. Destination: Java, the location of the old Batavia. The White Shadow wanted to be there to make sure nothing got in the way. There was too much at stake to rely on others. If necessary, he'd have to get his own hands dirty this time…

Belle screamed. The pirate had been lurking behind the door. Now he was launching himself at her, drawing his sabre. The bare bone of his skull was pressing on Belle's face, his long bony fingers reaching for her shoulder. Belle was about to scream again, when another hand covered her mouth.

"Not another sound!" Connor whispered in her ear. He grabbed the skeleton and sat it on a bench in the corner. Its drinking buddy was already perched there, a skeletal hand still clutching a tankard, even after over three hundred years.

Belle leaned on the door frame, panting as if she'd just run a marathon. She'd never been pounced on by a skeleton. Even if, technically, it had only tipped over onto her.

Oni put her hand on Belle's shoulder reassuringly. "It's a good sign," she said softly. "Malus and Tyron can't be in here already, otherwise the skeleton booby trap would have greeted them and not you."

"Great," Belle choked. "Good to know…"

Connor nodded. "So, this is where van Robbemond spent his days on land," he murmured. "Old Batavia – what a dump."

Finally, Belle found the strength to take a look around. Emmer Bloed was a single large room. The long bar extended along the wall, opposite the entrance. A few round-bodied bottles and stone tankards still stood on the shelves. A skeleton lay draped, face down, across the the bar, its torso crushed – this was probably the remains of the innkeeper.

In front of the innkeeper, on the floor, lay three overturned stools and a cluster of bones in torn clothing. The bare skulls that belonged to them were wrapped in bandanas.

Tables stood all around. One had been shattered by an enormous lump of rock – and so had the guests who'd been sitting at it. All that was left was a hand protruding from under the rock, holding a dice cup. Above them was a large hole in the ceiling, where the rock had hit during the earthquake. Connor looked through it.

"There aren't any rooms up there," he declared. "There's just the roof."

He swept the tankards and a knife from the next table and spread out the map with the letter on it.

"How did you get that?" asked Belle in astonishment.

"Well, I *do* have a few pickpockets' tricks up my sleeve, as it happens," Connor replied, grinning. "I took it out of Oliver's pocket before Tyron searched him."

Belle's face reddened, but Connor was concentrating on the map. Unfortunately, none of them could read the letter – Oliver was the only one who spoke Dutch.

"Van Robbemond is inviting Eleven-Fingered Louie to come to his chamber," he recalled. "So, where is it?"

Belle and Oni shrugged their shoulders.

"Shouldn't we look for Oliver and McFinnegan first?" Oni suggested.

Connor shook his head. "Why was the Phantom never caught?" he asked. "Because I always thought through every possibility in advance. We have to hope the two of them escape and come and find us in here."

Belle nodded.

"We need somewhere to hide," Connor explained. "I've searched the whole tavern. At the back, there's a tiny chamber with a bucket in it – the perfect double hiding place for little Fire Tigers." Connor grinned momentarily, but then carried on talking just as intensely. "Other than that – no doors, no stairs, no hatches in the floor. But van Robbemond definitely lived here, as we know from what he himself wrote, so his chamber must be hidden. And if we can't find it easily, then BONE certainly can't."

Belle scrunched up her face. "And Eleven-Fingered Louie neither..."

"Anubi!" Oni suddenly called out, her eyes darting around the room.

For a few heartbeats, the three of them held their breath. Then, to their relief, they heard a squeal. The meerkat had retreated into a side alcove that was separated from the bar room by a curtain full of holes.

Oni moved towards him, but stopped halfway.

"Connor, Belle, look at this!" she cried. "And bring the map with you!"

When Belle and Connor got to the alcove, Anubi was perched on the arm of a chair, scratching the wall with his little paws. The wall was covered in dirt, but Anubi's claws had exposed a small area, revealing a drawing of a nose and one closed eye. Belle recognised them from somewhere.

"It's the woman from the map!" Oni exclaimed. "The priestess with the headdress!"

Connor held the map up against the wall. The eyes and nose were identical. He pressed the map into Belle's hand and hurried back to the bar.

"Sorry, buddy, but I need that more than you do right now," he said, pulling the bandana off a skeleton's skull. He wound the material around his fist and began cleaning the dirt off the wall. More and more of the Indonesian woman became visible. She looked exactly like the woman on the map.

"That explains a few things," said Connor, throwing the bandana back to its bony owner. "I was wondering why van Robbemond would send a man like Eleven-Fingered Louie a map of old Batavia. If he really knew the Indonesian waters like the back of his hand, he must have been here plenty of times. So, the real signpost was the priestess, supposedly only drawn on the map for decoration." Connor knocked on the wooden wall. "So, this is the door to van Robbemond's chamber, where he was expecting Louie, Princess Li and Samson Mbeke on the first Sunday in April 1716."

Belle was astounded. Connor had remembered every detail of Oliver's translation whilst at the same time investigating the inner workings of the zeppelin. Slowly, it dawned on her why the Phantom had been so hard to catch: Connor wasn't just clever, but also, in every waking moment, highly alert. He must have learnt that right from an early age, when he started escaping from orphanages.

Now he was feeling along the wood panelling. "Here on the edges there are narrow cracks, but the handle is missing, unfortunately."

Oni had been studying the woman on the wall in silence while fondling Anubi's head. Now she also spoke up.

"Van Robbemond thought Eleven-Fingered Louie would understand the priestess clue," she said. "We don't know Louie's nationality, but he'd obviously been in Asia for a long time. So he should have been familiar with the different religions there. What do you notice about the woman?"

Connor listed her special features. "Her jewellery is lavish, which is why I thought she was a princess at first. And for some reason I get the feeling she is looking at me, even though her eyes are closed."

"And her make-up!" Belle realised. "Her elaborate eyeshadow and this dot on her forehead."

Oni nodded. "Some religions call this dot the Third Eye and believe real sight can only come from this…"

Oni lowered her voice as she spoke these last words. Now she raised one hand; she pressed two fingers on the closed eyes of the woman and her thumb on the Third Eye. Belle held her breath. The wood gave way under Oni's fingers, pushing inwards. The wood panelling disappeared into the adjacent wall.

Oni, Belle, Connor and Anubi crowded around the doorway. Before them stood the chamber of Bartholomeus van Robbemond. There was no question about it, for, staring down at them from the far wall of the chamber was the founder of the ACE. It was the same picture as the one hanging in the entrance hall of Deep Fog Castle.

Connor raised his hand to high-five the two girls. Belle joined in, but Oni shook her head.

"There are two reasons why we shouldn't celebrate yet," she said soberly. "Oliver has your lucky charm, and this chamber doesn't have any windows. It's not the right room."

"I'm going to take a look at it anyway," said Connor, taking a step forward while supporting himself on the door frame. As his hand moved away, it revealed three indentations in the wood.

Alarm bells went off in Belle's head. Her instinct always told her when something wasn't right, and it had saved her life a dozen times back in the Sahara. Without giving it a second thought, she dived at Connor and bundled him to the ground as three daggers flew out of the door frame and over his head, lodging in the indentations. Connor had escaped death by a hair's breadth.

"Thanks!" exclaimed Connor as he got up.

"You're welcome," Belle replied. "It was about time I had a go at saving a life."

Connor grinned. "Well, you're right there."

He switched on his torch and shone it on the floor in front of them. "Seems to be safe," he announced, "but take care, anyway."

Belle grinned. "Thanks for the tip – we'll do that."

Oni positioned a chair in the door-frame. "Now the door can't slam shut behind us and lock us in. Who knows what else van Robbemond thought up."

Belle was impressed by the way Oni seemed to think of everything. And how well she looked after Anubi. Oni had put the meerkat in her rucksack. Anubi didn't like it, but he gave in to his fate.

They couldn't see much in the room itself. Connor's torch flickered.

"Damn! Battery's out," he swore. "Give me my other torch."

Belle clenched her teeth. Connor had lent her his second torch in the warehouse. "It's still in the zeppelin," she said. "If I'd known the master thief didn't charge his batteries before every raid…"

Connor let out a long sigh. "Well, that's just great. What now?"

Oni pushed past him. "For goodness sake, let's light this candle!"

She rubbed a few leaves together in the air, and it

wasn't long before the candle on the table was burning. The candle stump was stuck to a skull with an eye patch, a few gold coins were lying around, and... Belle began to tremble. At the back, sitting on a chair, was...

She opened her mouth to scream, but she went into survival mode again. Her hand automatically covered her mouth. She panted in terror, trembling. She'd seen a whole host of skeletons today. But this one was more ghostly than all the others. It was wearing a dark uniform jacket with gleaming buttons. It had no shoes on and was staring at the door as if waiting desperately for guests. The skull, however, had been bashed by a large object. In one hand it was holding a sabre, and on the other it was wearing a big, sparkling ring. Another shudder ran down Belle's spine. The skeleton had eleven fingers.

"Eleven-fingered Louie," she choked. "So, he did find his way to van Robbemond. The earthquake surprised him, too."

"Let him rest in peace," Connor murmured. "Let's look for a clue to the temple instead. Maybe it didn't mean a window – maybe it meant a map or a drawing of the temple here in the chamber?"

Belle shook her head. How were they supposed to find anything here after three hundred years? Papers, and even leather hides with nautical charts inscribed on them would have disintegrated a long time ago in the damp conditions. And in any case, there wasn't all that much to investigate in the room itself: a bed, two chairs, the table, a few coins on the floor. Whatever else had been there before had disappeared. There was also a cupboard with broken shelves, which was set into a rock face. A heavy chest lay before it, sprung open, also on the floor. It was probably to this that Louie owed his bashed skull.

Once Belle had thoroughly examined the chest, she noticed Connor had gone quiet. He was standing in front of the portrait of van Robbemond, lost in thought, stroking a mole on his forearm. Suddenly, he came back to his senses and hastily pulled his sleeve down. Belle looked at the picture. Were her eyes deceiving her, or did van Robbemond have exactly the same mole?

"So, what now?" Connor asked.

That was when Belle realised what had been bothering her about the portrait this whole time. "The ring's missing!" she cried. "In the picture in the academy, van Robbemond is wearing a big ring, but in this picture he isn't. And why…?" Belle went over to the table. "Because Eleven-Fingered Louie has it!"

She stopped for a moment to enjoy the look of amazement on Oni's – and especially on Connor's – faces. But she was far from finished.

"Why did van Robbemond go to such lengths to make this chamber secure?" she asked.

"Because of the gold coins?" Oni suggested.

Connor shook his head. "No, van Robbemond had a reputation for being a dangerous pirate. No one would have risked making an enemy of him for the sake of a few coins. There must be something more valuable here. Something much, much, *much* more valuable."

"Exactly!" Belle agreed. She overcame her revulsion, took hold of Louie's finger and pulled off the ring. She took it over to the portrait. On van Robbemond's ring finger there was a barely visible slit. She pushed the band of the ring through. As it clicked into place, she turned the ring's stone so that it looked like the ring was on van Robbemond's finger. Right at that moment, the ground began to shake under their feet. With a groan, the cupboard with the rock face behind it swung to the side. They were met by a musty smell and a roughly hewn hole yawning at them like the jaws of a giant. Torches ignited along the corridor that ran beyond it.

"I don't believe it," Connor stammered, smiling at the others. "We've found a secret passage!"

Belle shook her head. “Well, I found it, but you’re still very welcome to—”

Belle stopped mid-sentence. Voices were coming from outside Emmer Bloed.

“You’ve been leading us on a wild goose chase for long enough, kid,” Malus snarled. “Where is van Robbemond’s chamber?”

The door of the tavern was thrust open. They were coming! Belle could already see Tyron’s grimacing face through the tattered curtain. Oliver and McFinnegan were with them, dirty but unharmed. With much bluster, they entered the Bucket Full of Blood. It was too late to slam the chamber door shut. They had no other choice but to try to escape: through the tunnel…

The Escape

Belle hurried onwards. She could hear Oni's and Connor's steps behind her, echoing off the walls three times as loud. Quite a way off, she could hear Malus swearing. They'd put a good hundred metres between themselves and the villains from BONE. Too few to feel safe yet, but sufficient to be able to think clearly. The tunnel was just high enough for Belle not to keep hitting her head on it. A tall man like Malus wouldn't be able to get down this tunnel as quickly as they could, so they had an advantage. It rankled with Belle that she had done the hard work for Malus and Tyron. They would never have found the secret entrance on their own – Belle was certain of that. But at least McFinnegan and Oliver were nearby again. That was one teeny-tiny worry fewer…

Belle ran and ran. How much further did this tunnel go? And where was it leading, anyway? Was it just an escape route to the outside? Belle doubted that. It had been too well protected for just that, as they had already established. And then this ingenious system with the torches. How had van Robbemond got the things to turn on by themselves? Every five steps, there was one hanging on the wall. So far. Although, suddenly everything in front of Belle was dark.

"Stop!" she called, coming to a halt. That gut instinct again. Belle had a feeling something was wrong.

"Give me the last torch, Connor," she commanded. Behind her, a torch was wrenched from the wall, and as she held it aloft, the ground before her feet lit up.

"I knew it!" Belle exclaimed. Only a metre in front of them lay a pit. It was too wide to jump over. As Belle, Connor and Oni approached the edge, the bottom of the pit began to move. Snakes! Provoked by the unusual light, their mouths opened wide, revealing their long, poisoned fangs. The little bones dotted around proved they hadn't forgotten how to use them.

"Urgh!" Belle groaned. She wasn't the kind of girl to be scared of creepy-crawlies or anything that spun a web. But the thought of having come within a hair's breadth of falling into this pit was anything but pleasant.

"Psst!" said Oni, her amulet glowing. "We won't hurt you."

The reptiles did seem to calm down, but that didn't

solve their problem, for Malus and Tyron were still coming ever closer.

Connor unfastened his rucksack and took out a reel of thick wire rope. He aimed it at the ceiling over the pit and shot a hook out from it. With a cracking sound, the metal bored into the rock. Connor pulled on the rope.

"Absolutely secure," he said. "Who wants to go first?"

He held the end of the rope out towards Oni, who grabbed it with both hands. "Absolutely secure, right?" she asked. Without waiting for an answer, she swung over the pit. Once on the other side, she sent the rope back again. Belle was next.

"Leave the torch there so the others don't fall in," Belle called out to Connor, when she was safely across.

Connor nodded. "Although I'd gladly let two of them take their chances…" When he landed on the other side, he pressed a button on the reel and the rope wound itself up again.

"Stop right there, or the Scotsman will get it!" roared Malus behind them.

"Who's bothered about teachers?" replied Belle with an artificial laugh. She hoped McFinnegan wouldn't hold it against her.

After a bend in the tunnel, there were torches on the walls again. This meant Belle could see the thick spiders' webs blocking their way. Was she mistaken, or were eight eyes watching them though a crevice in the rock?

"Let me do it," said Oni. "Spiders' webs bring luck. If you put them on fresh wounds, they heal twice as quickly."

Gently, as if they were little works of art, she brushed the threads to the side, singing a song with a sweet melody. Was it a lullaby to send the spiders to sleep?

Now Connor was running on ahead. The tunnel was growing higher and wider, but a pile of debris was blocking the way. It must have broken off in the earthquake. Connor climbed up onto it and started rolling the boulders to the side. Once he'd made a large hole, he squeezed through.

"Oh!" came the sound from the other side. Then there was silence.

"Connor?" called Belle. "Is everything okay?"

"Yes, yes!" Connor rejoiced. "Come on! Hurry up! You have to see this!"

Oni took off her rucksack, with Anubi still in it, and passed it through to Connor. Then she too left the tunnel.

When Belle poked her head through, she was lost for words. She'd never seen anything like it in all her life!

The secret passage led into a gigantic cave. The cave was so high that it could have housed three Deep Fog Castles, one on top of another. It seemed to be raining from the jagged ceiling, but it was only condensation,

for, twenty metres below them, the sea was sloshing about. It must have found its way into the cave through underground inlets, for all around them there was nothing but rock. The sunlight shone in through circular holes, illuminating a ship with three masts – van Robbemond's flag was flying from it, and on the prow, still resplendent in pitch-black lettering, was the name *Hollandia*.

"How did that get in here?" Belle stammered, slipping right through into the cave. "And is this why van Robbemond was never caught? He and his ship could just disappear altogether, like a phantom." Belle laughed. "Could be an ancestor of yours, Connor."

Connor didn't laugh along with her.

"We have to go aboard the *Hollandia* – that much is obvious," he muttered. Before either of the girls could reply, he was already leaping down the stone steps into the bay. They ended on a narrow strip of sand forming a bridge over to the ship.

"Come on, let's follow him," Belle prompted Oni. When Oni didn't move, Belle took her hand. It was cold and clammy.

"We'll soon be outside, and you'll see the sky again," she promised Oni. Belle hoped this was true.

When they caught up with Connor, he'd already pulled himself on board by a thick rope. He was standing at the back of the ship. He looked down at them and greeted them like a captain.

"Fancy playing pirates?" he called out, grinning.

The rope was suspended from a hoist. Connor gave it a shove, and Belle grabbed it. The lower end was slippery and covered in algae. Belle took a deep breath and swung off. She managed to climb up the rope, only getting her shoes wet. Once Oni had climbed up unscathed too, Connor knelt beside the ship's wheel.

"Look at that!" he said reverently. "It looks like van Robbemond invented a kind of autopilot. There are pictures of different destinations scorched into the ring of the wheel, and the same pictures are on the beam beside it – one of them is a temple with a burning tiger!"

Connor tried to turn the wheel so that both the pictures of the temple were at the same height. But it didn't move an inch.

"You should know by now that van Robbemond wouldn't have been as careless as that," said Oni. "To set the destination, you need a key, and there's a different key for each one. Here!"

She ran her slim fingers over deep indentations on the beam. Next to each destination was a differently shaped indentation. Belle, too, had noticed this, but thought they were just decoration. Beside the temple was a semicircle with a jagged line. There was a little indentation in the line.

"Connor's lucky charm!" Oni, Connor and Belle cried simultaneously.

"The coin isn't a signpost – it's a key!" exclaimed Belle.

"So, now the time has come to free Oliver and McFinnegan," Connor declared. "They've been holding Malus and Tyron off for long enough. Are you ready to trick BONE?"

Belle clenched her fists. "I've never been more ready for anything!"

Destination: Temple of the Fire Tiger

Belle was lying under a sailcloth trying not to breathe. The beam was pressing on her stomach, but that's the way it had to be. To Malus and Tyron it had to look like she, Connor and Oni had blundered into a trap and been struck dead by a falling mast. But would it work?

BONE are dangerous criminals! Oliver's words were spinning round in Belle's head like a carousel.

"Where are they, then?" whispered Belle. "We got rid of all the obstacles in their way!"

"Sssh!" hissed Connor. "They're coming!"

Suddenly Belle heard it, too. First, Malus's piercing voice, then Tyron, growling.

"Not a soul in sight," the thug declared. "Nice friends you've got, I must say. Just legged it. Couldn't give a damn about the teacher – not even about young four-eyes here."

Oliver howled. Belle hoped he was exaggerating it so

they'd underestimate him and think he was just a cry-baby.

"But they led us to the ship," called Malus, with a whistle through his teeth. "Clever idea to hide the galleon in here – you've got to give it to van Robbemond. Could have come straight out of Diablo Cortez's book."

It seemed like an eternity before Malus, Tyron, McFinnegan and Oliver finally climbed on board. Suddenly, Belle felt someone grab her hand, lift it up, then drop it back down onto the planks.

"Stone dead, all three of them!" declared Tyron, laughing. "Take a good look – you're next!"

Belle could only see the villain's boots. He was standing in the right place.

"Now!" she gave the command, letting go of the rope in her other hand. A barrel filled with water hurtled down the side of the ship, and its weight heaved the sail and the beam into the air. Oni, Belle and Connor all leapt up together. The beam, which a moment ago had been resting on their bodies, was now hovering in the air, one metre above the planks. Belle gave it a firm push. It shot forwards and hit Tyron in the stomach.

The gangster lost his balance and fell overboard with a splash. While Malus stood there, bewildered, Connor seized the opportunity to drive him backwards towards a trip-wire. The villain's shoe got caught, then, cursing and flapping his arms about wildly, he tumbled into the water too.

"Have you hauled in all the ropes?" Connor called.

Oni and Belle nodded, and only then did they greet McFinnegan and Oliver.

"Wow!" exclaimed Oliver in amazement. "What a cool trap. I also thought something had happened to you at first."

Connor jokingly got Oliver in a headlock, clamping him tight. "You're one hell of a guy!" he gushed. "Making out you're so innocent and leading the gangsters on a wild goose chase."

Oliver laughed. "Ow, ow, get off, that hurts!" he howled exaggeratedly again, then laughed once more. "Sounds real, doesn't it?"

"Are you okay too, Mr McFinnegan?" Belle asked.

Her teacher nodded. "I've no idea how to explain any of this to Catherine, but otherwise, yes, I think I'm still in good shape. To be honest, I feel twenty years younger than before we set off on this journey."

The teacher peered over the bulwark. "I don't want to rush things, but the Alex Malus I know won't give up so easily. We ought to get going."

Connor didn't pay him any attention.

"Oliver, have you got my coin?"

Oliver took it out of his pocket.

"It's a key for the wheel," Connor explained. "Here, can you see this cavity? That's where you insert it."

Red-faced with excitement, Oliver took Connor's lucky charm and pushed it firmly into the hole.

At the same time, Connor pulled the wheel round, and this time it was easy to turn. Once the pictures on the wheel and the beam were aligned, the rudder engaged.

"What now?" Oliver asked.

Barely had he uttered the question, when a jolt went through the ship. The galleon pushed off from the sand, and the anchor hauled itself in. Launched as if by magic, the ship set off, steering inch by inch towards the rock face!

"What's going on?" cried Belle. "Is this one of van Robbemond's traps, too?"

A thunderous crunching sounded though the cave. The rocks were quaking and trembling. The sea was foaming at the prow of the ship, but there was still no obvious way out.

"The rocks over there are a gateway," Oliver called. "They moved apart when the galleon set off. But the mechanism is jamming. It must be from the earthquake!"

Belle bit her lower lip. The ship started building up

speed. In only a few minutes it would smash against the wall, at the same time shattering any hope of finding the temple!

Then, to make matters worse, Anubi started screeching at the top of his voice.

“Connor, Belle!” cried Oni. “They’re coming on board!”

Belle followed her voice. Oni was standing one deck below, looking out through a porthole. Anubi was hopping around agitatedly on the cannon behind her.

Malus was clambering up the side of the ship. He was only a few metres away from them.

“Get away from the porthole!” Connor roared suddenly.

When Belle turned around, she saw the burning fuse on the rear side of the cannon. She threw herself on Oni, and the two of them fell to the floor.

Then came a crash and the sound of wood splitting. Belle felt a draught at her back. When she stood up again, there was a huge hole in the side of the ship. Ten metres below them, something landed with a splash in the water. Alexander Malus! The cannonball struck the rock face, sending debris crashing down to the shoreline.

“That’s it!” cried Connor. “Anubi, you’re worth your weight in gold!”

The three of them rushed back on deck. Up at the front, on the prow, were three large cannons.

"We'll shoot our way out!" declared Connor. "Aim for the mechanism!"

Soon after, cannonballs were crashing, one by one. They used van Robbemond's rapid firelighters, so they didn't need to reload powder or light fuses. They'd barely loaded a cannonball into the gun barrel before it was off, speeding through the cave. One after the other bored into the rock face before them. Huge chunks of rock rained down. But not a ray of sunlight was coming through, and the ship was moving unflinchingly onwards.

Even McFinnegan was rolling cannonballs out from the deepest recesses of the ship. A particularly heavy one dropped into the water just short of its target. Right at that moment, a jolt went through the rocks. They ground, creaked and groaned, then moved apart. The way was clear.

"Oni, you hit it!" Oliver rejoiced.

Oni climbed up on the gun barrel and stretched out her arms. Fresh air streamed towards them, ruffling Oni's curls even more.

Belle stood beside her and took a deep breath. The galleon pushed slowly out of the cave. The sails unfurled and immediately swelled with wind. If their club founder's autopilot invention still worked, they were now on course. And at the speed the ship was going, it would only take a few days to reach any destination in the world.

Belle could feel all the pressure of the last few hours lifting. Now she felt three things at once: hunger, thirst and tiredness. She hadn't eaten or drunk anything for a long time, and she could barely remember what a bed looked like.

Belle looked back again at the mouth of the cave. Two tiny figures were standing there, flapping their arms about wildly. The curses that were most definitely coming out of their mouths were being swallowed by the wind.

In the Jungle

The ship granted its five and a half passengers an afternoon and a whole night of downtime. No one turned the wheel or sat in the crow's nest, and still the galleon cut through the waves like a knife through butter.

The first thing Oliver had done was construct a sea-water filter system out of a sailcloth and a few pots. Soon, they had enough fresh water to quench their collective thirst.

McFinnegan had contacted TICI to get the Sky Explorer to follow them in camouflage mode. TICI had even let down one of Oliver's bags. It contained parts of the thoughtophone. After Oliver had studied the rudder and the rapid-fire cannons in detail, he tried to rebuild the broken machine. In the late afternoon, he presented the others with an enhanced version. Now the device fitted comfortably in his trouser pocket. Oliver had built two of them.

"They work like walkie-talkies," he explained. "Only, without batteries or cables. You just think of the other person and then you can talk to them."

Connor spent hours inspecting the ship. On two occasions, Belle came upon him sitting at van Robbemond's card table in the captain's cabin, repeatedly stroking the mole on his arm, lost in thought.

Oni was just enjoying the open sky above her hammock. Anubi had made friends with a seagull, and the two of them were chasing each other around the deck.

Belle also tried to take a midday nap, but whenever she closed her eyes, a skeleton appeared before her. Fortunately, there weren't any here on board – or at least, they hadn't found any. Nonetheless, Belle always carried a sabre with her now. She'd found it in a cupboard in the captain's cabin. You could never be too sure whether dead pirates were cursed or not…

As darkness fell, McFinnegan asked TICI to send down a basket of food on a rope, then he made a big pot of soup in the ship's galley. "An old Scottish family recipe!" he announced proudly.

They ate the soup on deck. Anubi had cuddled up to Oni in her lap and gone to sleep. Beside them was the glow of an old lamp, above them millions of stars, and all around them the smell of sea and old wood.

“Do you know anything about the other founders of the ACE?” Belle asked eventually.

McFinnegan stroked his beard for a long time before answering.

“No more than were listed in the letter,” he began. “There was another pirate with eleven fingers, an adventurous princess from China, and a fellow from Northern Africa who was much taller than the average man. They each owned a magical object that only worked when all four of them were together.”

The old Scotsman took a sip of Oliver’s water. “It was clearly van Robbemond’s idea to found a club for adventurers, but the ACE became legendary in the first three years because they all worked together. Then, around 1719, the stories about the four of them just stopped.

Connor nodded. “And now we know why,” he declared. “During the earthquake in old Batavia, Eleven-Fingered Louie was guarding the entrance to the cave. A chest fell from the cupboard and bashed his skull. His magical object became worthless, which means the other three did, too.”

Oni stretched out her arms. “I have to go to sleep,” she mumbled, “but before I do, I still want to know one thing. What kind of objects were they?”

McFinnegan laughed. "The ACE has been trying to solve this mystery since the death of its founder. But van Robbemond didn't record anything about it. Maybe you'll find something in his logbook."

"Yes…" Belle replied, her eyelids closing, "tomorrow…"

When Belle opened her eyes again, the sun was shining on her face. The ship was floating calmly on the water. Somewhere, a monkey shrieked.

Belle sat up. Although she'd been lying on the ship's hard planks all night, she felt as fresh as a daisy, livelier than she'd felt for a long time.

But… Belle was alone on deck – where were the others?

"Connor? Oni? Oliver?" she called. "Mr McFinnegan?"

With the sabre in her hand, she hurried over to the bulwark and looked down. Ten metres below, the four of them were standing on the shore of a river surrounded by giant plants. They were waving to her. There was nothing to see but jungle far and wide.

"Come on, sleepy head," Connor teased her. "Oliver's discovered a signpost to the temple!"

Belle put the sabre between her teeth like a real pirate and clambered all the way down the anchor chain. Soon, she was up to her waist in water. The bath refreshed her! When she got to the others, Anubi greeted her like an old friend.

Oliver was kneeling in front of a stone structure in the shape of a square beacon. At the top and bottom was a square platform. Oliver was examining the signs on the sides of the stone with a magnifying glass. Belle knelt beside it. The stone was covered in symbols, but not any kind she'd seen before.

"Hmm, I can't make head nor tail of these," she said after a while.

"They're universal signs – a person from South America would have understood these, too," McFinnegan explained. "This building here means a temple, the sun and the morning star indicate the compass direction, and the skull and crossbones… Well, you've probably worked that one out for yourselves: beware!"

Belle felt her stomach churn. She'd seen far too many skulls and crossbones over the past few days.

"So, the temple's this way," Oliver concluded from the signs, pointing straight into the jungle.

McFinnegan nodded. "That's how I read it, too. But… I'm not coming with you. I'm going to go back to the Sky Explorer. You'll need someone covering you from the air, and I can come down and extract you if necessary." He held up the thoughtophone. "Thanks to Oliver, of course, we can keep in touch easily – and we know it's bug-proof."

Belle, Oni, Connor and Oliver agreed.

"Is there anything else we should know?" Connor asked. "I always gather as much information as I can about the place I'm, well… *working* in."

McFinnegan wiped the sweat from his brow. A three-piece tweed suit really wasn't the most suitable clothing for this hot and humid climate.

"I'll give you the legend of the Fire Tiger to take along with you," the teacher replied, sitting down on a fallen tree. "Once upon a time, a little boy rescued a baby tiger from a forest fire. From then on, the two were inseparable. Many years later, the boy's tribe was attacked, and the tiger died trying to protect the boy."

Belle saw Oni burying her nose in Anubi's fur. Her roommate really was very sensitive – Belle liked this character trait in Oni immensely.

"The boy was driven half-mad with grief and rage," McFinnegan continued. "Wanting revenge, he asked the gods for help. He was told he should make a big fire, out of which the tiger would rise from the dead. The boy followed this suggestion, and the spirit of the tiger really did rise up out of the flames. In its jaws it held a dagger, which it gave to the boy. The boy used it to defend his village against further attacks. Eventually, he was chosen as chieftain of the tribe and given the title of the Tiger King. His people were called Tiger Warriors. After the death of the Tiger King, many people fought over the dagger – they wanted to use its power for themselves. So, a priestess hid the indestructible dagger in her temple in the jungle in order to stop it falling into the wrong hands."

Oliver nodded. "But we know something else from another source," he added, lowering his voice. "The priestess swore an oath after the death of the Tiger King: she would never sleep as long as there was something to guard on the altar. She's been living in the Tiger Temple for over five hundred years." Oliver ran his finger over the drawing of the priestess on the map. "Apart from van Robbemond, no one has ever returned from the Temple of the Fire Tiger."

The Temple of the Fire Tiger

Sweat was pouring down Belle's back; her T-shirt was clinging to her body. She was also being used as a landing pad by insects that were longer than her index finger.

The path that Oliver had chosen to take led diagonally through the jungle. It didn't look like anyone at all had been here since van Robbemond's times. To make matters worse, it was all uphill. For most of the journey, Belle had been leading the troops, slashing a pathway through with the sabre. Oni clapped for joy whenever an armadillo or lizard burst out of the bushes. Even the sight of a toad the size of a football seemed to delight her.

"This is paradise itself!" she kept saying, jubilantly.

Connor said nothing. Whenever the going got tough, he could completely withdraw into himself and overcome any hurdle. His body moved forwards while his spirit rested.

Then, after almost three hours of hiking, Connor stopped at an enormous hill in the middle of the forest. He leaned on a rock and caught his breath.

"Erm… Connor…" squeaked Oliver suddenly. "You might just want to check what you're leaning against…"

Connor moved away in slow motion and took gradual steps backwards.

Protruding from the dense bush was the mouth of a beast. The teeth were as sharp as nails, and milky-yellow – but the animal didn't move.

Belle thought for a moment, then slashed the plants a few times with her blade.

"A tiger," she declared. "Made of stone."

"There's another one over here," said Oliver. "And between them… the entrance to a temple!"

Oliver did battle with a tenacious climbing plant, but eventually he managed to yank it down from the stones. Behind it stood a walled gate. The stones above and to the sides fitted so snugly together that there were barely any gaps between them. The builders of the temple had chiselled symbols into the stone, but even Belle couldn't decipher their meaning.

"Could be a warning," she suggested.

Either way, she would rather have known exactly what was awaiting her in the temple – apart from a five-hundred-year-old woman haunting the place…

"We're going in," Connor announced over the thoughtophone to McFinnegan.

"All right," it rattled back. "If you're not back in an hour, I'll start looking for you. Over."

"Over," murmured Belle, pensively.

"Hang on," whispered Oni. "Do you really want to go in there?"

Every part of Belle recoiled from this. She thought of the four-poster bed in the academy, her parents, and the argument with her dad on the day of the ceremony. She didn't want to die. But…

"We have no choice," she said, her voice trembling. "If BONE gets its hands on the ruby, it'll be the end of the world. We have to risk it."

"Exactly!" said Connor, spurring her on. "We've made it this far – we can tackle the rest too! I believe in us!"

Belle nodded. She'd longed for adventures, and now she was right in the middle of the biggest adventure she'd ever imagined. No, it was actually *much* bigger than Belle could ever have imagined. She wasn't going to back down now. And she most definitely wasn't going to die. Not today, and not here.

Belle took a step into the temple, and the temperature immediately dropped to pleasantly cool. The thick walls were keeping the scorching heat at bay. But it was dark. There were no self-igniting torches here. Made sense – after all, ghosts didn't like the light.

Despite the darkness, the area beside Belle suddenly lit up. Connor had a stick in his hand that was giving off colourful sparks.

"It's actually an emergency flare for if you need help in the mountains," Connor explained matter-of-factly. "I adapted it a bit, and now you can use it as an extra-strong light."

For Anubi, who was back in Oni's rucksack, the light was clearly too dazzling. He scrunched his eyes up, and it wasn't long before he fell asleep. Everyone else kept their eyes open, but there were no traps, hidden trapdoors or snake pits here. The corridor led straight into the temple. In the walled alcoves to the left and right stood one figure after another. They all resembled the priestess on the map, but each had its own facial features. Was one of them the guardian, and was she watching them?

Eventually, the four comrades came to a stop before an

altar. On top stood an open casket lined with lily-white silk. A single ruby lay on the material.

"That was easy!" laughed Belle, and was about to pick it up when Connor grabbed her arm.

"Too easy," he warned. "Take it from a master thief: you don't just find valuable things lying around like that. They're always protected, visibly or invisibly."

Belle's face contorted in fear. She looked left, right, up and down, but she didn't notice anything out of the ordinary.

"The story of the guardian was obviously a fairy tale. There's nothing here..."

Belle fell silent. Behind the altar was an elaborately decorated archway that led deeper into the temple. A loud growling was coming from behind it. Belle took a step backwards, and everyone crowded together. Nothing at all happened for a few moments. Then, an enormous tiger emerged from the passageway. Unfortunately, it wasn't made of stone but of flesh and blood. It was very much alive, yet its fur was burning without burning up! Belle held her breath.

The Fire Tiger slunk around the altar, then positioned itself, threateningly, right in front of the casket with the ruby in it. It stared at the intruders, its eyes flashing.

"I think I know now why there are no traps," Oliver

whispered. “Whoever comes in here will be gobbled up anyway.”

Oni pushed through her friends to get to the front. She raised her hands reassuringly, then began saying something incomprehensible to the fearsome beast. Her amulet was glowing brighter than ever before. But the tiger would not be pacified. It growled again, lashing out at Oni with its paw.

“Stay calm…!” Oni whispered. “We have not come to do evil. Quite the contrary. Evil people want to take the ruby. And then there will be a disaster!”

The tiger roared so loudly that stones rained down from the ceiling onto the foursome.

“Mmmmm… D-do you think…” Oliver stammered, “do you think it would disturb the Fire Tiger if we took a photo of it?”

Belle ignored him. She’d noticed something about the tiger. “Do you see the dot on its forehead?” she whispered. “The Third Eye? I’m sure the tiger is a tigress… Oliver, what exactly was the oath the priestess swore?”

Oliver trembled from head to toe. “She… she wouldn’t sleep as long as there was something to guard on the altar.”

“Are you sure?” Belle pressed him further.

"Yes, yes, that's what my grandmother always told me," Oliver repeated. "She loved the story..."

Belle nodded. "Then I know what we need to do. Connor, you shoot a hook with a rope into the ceiling directly above the altar. Oni, you distract the tigress. She mustn't look up. And Oliver, you help Connor!" Belle took a deep breath. "I'm going to get the ruby."

When Belle turned round, she saw horror in Oliver's eyes and admiration in Connor's.

"Okay," he said quietly. "That's what we'll do."

Belle had never before seen a look like the one that was in Oni's eyes. Oni was concentrating all her attention on the tigress. "You're a girl, aren't you?" said Oni in a gentle voice. She knelt, then sat down cross-legged. The guardian looked down at her.

"Now!" hissed Belle.

Instantly, Connor shot the hook out of the reel, and it bored almost soundlessly into the solid rock. One end of the rope was in the reel, the other was fastened to a special belt hanging out of Connor's rucksack. Belle put it on.

"Okay, we're hoisting you up," whispered Connor. He and Oliver pitted themselves against Belle's weight and wound the reel. Belle was lifted up from the floor.

"Good girl..." she heard Oni say.

By now she was swaying above the altar.

The boys released the rope gradually. Belle twisted round in the belt so that her feet were pointing upwards. Three metres, two metres, one...

When Belle's outstretched fingers were almost touching the ruby, the tigress leapt up. She turned and stared at Belle. The flames on her back were blazing brightly.

"Keep going!" Belle screamed. "More rope!"

She hurtled downwards and nearly fell onto the altar.

The tigress leapt. At the same time, Belle grabbed the ruby.

"Up! Pull me up!"

Once Belle was hovering above the tigress at a safe distance, she showed her the ruby. "I've got it!" she cried out to the beast. "There's nothing left on the altar for you to guard. You have fulfilled your oath..."

The tigress leapt at her. Belle curled up to protect herself, but the tigress's fire went out mid-flight. Her contours blurred, she became smaller and more delicate, and her fur receded, revealing a robe made of silk. When the guardian landed on the altar, her paws had become hands and feet – and the tigress had become the priestess from van Robbemond's drawing.

“It’s just as Bartholomeus predicted!” said the priestess, getting to her feet. “The four will appear and outwit you together. They will come to take what is destined to be theirs.”

The servant began to fade; her voice was ebbing away. “Four children, four objects. Four, like my loyal friends and I – Samson, Louie, Li and me.”

“Hey!” cried Belle from up above. “Don’t go! What objects? What four objects?”

But the woman didn’t reply. She had disappeared into thin air, taking the light from the temple with her.

There was silence for a moment. It was as if Connor, Belle, Oliver and Oni were spellbound. None of them wanted to destroy this magic with words.

It was Connor who finally broke the silence.

“It doesn’t matter what she meant,” he said, slowly letting Belle down. “The main thing is, we have the ruby.”

“Very true!” an unpleasantly shrill voice came through the temple. “You have the ruby. And you can exchange it for the life of a friend.”

Stunned, Belle came down from the altar. A large chest was blocking their way out of the temple. As she came closer, Belle realised it was a sedan chair, in which kings used to be carried through the streets. The two chairbearers puffed and panted – Alex Malus and Tyron. And in the sedan sat a man whose skin glowed snow-white in the darkness. McFinnegan was slumped beside him.

A pale hand extended towards Belle from the gloom, and in a calm voice that would tolerate no contradiction, the man said, “The ruby for his life!”

The Four Appear

Belle, Oni, Oliver und Connor were crouching on the steps before the altar. By now, they knew that the man with the pale skin was called Alfred P. Hades but nicknamed the White Shadow, and that he was the head of BONE. They knew that Malus had planted a bug on van Robbemond's ship. They knew that he and Tyron had followed them in a mechanical dolphin. They knew that the two of them had caught McFinnegan off guard on the Sky Explorer and dragged him into the sedan chair. And they knew they had no other option but to hand the ruby over to the White Shadow.

Hades climbed down from the sedan chair.

"Thank you for saving me a lot of work," Hades said unctuously. "I anticipated some things, you surprised me with others – but one can allow for surprises too, as I'm sure the Phantom will agree."

Belle sensed Connor twitching uneasily beside her.

Connor felt BONE had robbed him of his honour – he'd never made a secret of this.

"Breaking contracts is no surprise," Connor bellowed into the darkness. "Saying one thing and doing another is dishonourable!"

"Ooooh!" the White Shadow crowed with glee. "You have principles – how sweet. But I'm not here to play the man of honour. I'm going to take over the world, and I'm going to do so using the ruby you're going to give to me, pretty little Belle, right now."

Belle was livid. Whenever anyone judged her by her appearance – or even decided she was stupid – she always felt she was about to explode.

"First you have to let our teacher go," Belle replied, her voice trembling.

The White Shadow was silent for a moment. Then they could see him click his fingers in the air.

"Alexander, bring your favourite teacher over here," he ordered. "But the little blondie didn't specify that all his fingers should remain in place…"

Malus laughed, but Belle reckoned he didn't have the stomach for it. Tyron was the one who broke fingers – not Alex Malus. "Here he is. Should I…"

"Stop, right where you are," Hades commanded Malus. "Now come here, girl. Give Mr Tyron the ruby."

Belle stood up and went over to Tyron the Tyrant.

"Slowly!" rasped Alfred P. Hades, looking each of them in the eye in turn. "No tricks, promise?"

"Promise!" replied Connor, Oliver, Oni and Belle in unison.

"Very well, carry on."

Belle was in two minds. Maybe she should… No. Whatever she decided to do would be wrong.

But Tyron made the decision for her. His powerful hand shot out, twisted Belle's arm around and squeezed the jewel from her hand.

"Ow!" Belle shrieked, tears in her eyes.

"Stop messing about, Tyron," the White Shadow ordered. "And you, Alexander, let the fool go."

Belle wrestled herself free from Tyron and found her way back to the others.

"Thank you," sneered Hades. "And while you're all together and having such a nice time, we might as well test our new wonder weapon. Tyron, the ruby! Alex, the dagger, s'il vous plaît!"

Tyron moved towards the White Shadow. Alexander Malus hurried over to the sedan chair. "Where…?" he stammered. "It should be…?" The panic was rising in Alex Malus's voice. "The dagger's not there!"

"Close your eyes!" Connor cried.

There was a cracking sound at their feet and a flash of piercing light – Belle could see the flash, even through closed eyes. And it smelled like the little white cloud that appeared out of nowhere that time when she first came across Connor backstage. The White Shadow roared. In pain, but doubtless also in fury.

"Run!" Connor hissed at the others. Further into the temple!" Belle opened her eyes again. In one hand Connor held another emergency flare – and in the other the glinting Fire Tiger!

Belle immediately set off running. Oliver and McFinnegan were in front of her, Oni at her side with Anubi. Connor ran on ahead with the torch. He kept hurling little pellets backwards over their heads, which produced more clouds and reduced the visibility for their pursuers. Belle leapt over countless skeletons lying on the floor.

Finally, the passageway ended at a deep, wide shaft. A stone spiral staircase led downwards, but its steps were barely any wider than car tyres. If you missed a step, you'd hurtle one hundred metres down into the depths.

"Don't overthink it! Just take each step as quickly as you can!" Connor cried.

"Yes," Oliver moaned, "but we also don't want to end up as worm food..."

But when he heard Tyron's voice in the passageway, he set off down the staircase. Even McFinnegan managed it.

At the bottom though, five minutes later, their escape was blocked by a stone gate. It was completely covered in the same universal signs as the stone beacon Oliver had found in the jungle.

"Can you interpret this too?" Connor pressed McFinnegan.

The teacher tipped his head back. "Hmm, difficult," he mumbled, out of breath. "Four – the number four keeps coming up… feet and weapons, plants, and a needle pointing to the sky… I can't work it out…"

Belle turned around. Tyron and Malus were only twenty steps from the bottom. There had to be a solution…

And then she saw it. On the floor. Across the entire room, the floor slabs went from the wall on the left to the wall on the right in one continuous sequence. But right in front of the gate, four red slabs had been embedded in the grey stone.

"The four will appear!" Belle repeated the words of the priestess. "Each of us must stand on a different slab, quickly!"

McFinnegan, Oni and Connor each stood on a slab.

"But there are five of us!" protested Oliver, looking helplessly at Belle.

"So, this is where your escape ends," Belle heard Tyron wheeze behind her.

She took a run-up and leapt onto Oliver's back. Oliver stumbled forwards slightly onto the fourth red slab. Right at that moment, the stone gate slid to the side. Connor, Oni, McFinnegan and Oliver with his human rucksack rushed through, into the room beyond. And before the gangsters could follow them, the gate closed again.

Belle slid down from Oliver's back. They were all too amazed to speak.

The room was three storeys high and completely empty apart from a stone plinth with a chest on it. Someone,

however, had drawn directly onto the walls. Belle's expertise told her instantly that these drawings were not Javanese, but European. There were nautical charts plotted with the best waterways. There were illustrations of gleaming golden goose eggs, the magic drum of an Indian chieftain, a lamp with a genie coming out of it, chicken feet in the hands of a voodoo priest, clocks with numbers the wrong way round, a mammoth in a block of ice, and hundreds of other peculiar objects and artefacts. Considering Bartholomeus's interest in magical artefacts, he probably drew these himself.

"Look at this!" Oliver cried suddenly. He was standing in the middle of the room, in front of the plinth. "The chest here has ACE engraved on it."

Oni was the first to get to him. "Locked," she confirmed. "And there's no way I'm going back out again to look for the key."

Belle gave it some thought. But it didn't take long.

"You don't need one," she said. "Connor, give me the Fire Tiger."

Belle inserted the dagger into the lock and turned it. The lid sprang open and the four children were bathed in light. The thoughtophone started up in Oliver's bag.

"Welcome to the four of you. You have finally

appeared," said a voice from the device. "Only by combining your strengths did you manage to solve the mysteries, overcome the difficulties and get this far. Your destiny is to guard the secrets of the Adventure Club of Europe."

"Is… is it… van Robbemond?" whispered Oliver. "Inside my invention?"

"In this chest you will find four objects full of magic – one from each of us, for each of you. Oliver, my compass is for you. It will always show you when there are objects nearby that are connected with big mysteries."

Oliver reached into the chest and reverently took out a compass with countless pointers, needles and cogs. He was all smiles.

"Oni, the leather bag belonging to Samson Mbeke is for you. It is equipped with all kinds of medicinal herbs, and it keeps on replenishing itself."

Oni had to gulp three times before she felt ready to take the bag out of the chest.

"Belle Pompadour, the rapier belonging to Princess Li is for you. In the hands of a master fighter like you, it is more than a weapon. It will become a true ally."

Belle took a deep breath. As she bent over the chest, she felt the light from inside it on her face, soothing and warm. She lifted out the rapier and held it in her hands. It was as light as a feather, its handle elaborately decorated. As Belle sliced the air with its blade, she felt her arm tingling. It was almost as if the weapon was alive and she already had a deep bond with it.

"Thank you!" whispered Belle in awe, thinking of Princess Li.

"Connor Blaze, there is a pair of shoes for you. They are the wonderboots that belonged to my friend, Eleven-Fingered Louie. When wearing these, you can sneak around without making a single sound."

Connor took the boots out of the chest and bowed.

"These artefacts will only work for you – and only when you are together. This is to ensure, in the spirit of me and my comrades, that you stick together and work in the best interests of the club, as we founders of the ACE once did." Van Robbemond laughed. "And in case you don't know where to start, look around this room. All these mysteries and many more are already waiting for you to solve them…"

Laughter came from the thoughtophone once more, then there was silence. For a long time, no one said a word. There was a reverent atmosphere in the room, and later on they would all say that this was the moment their indestructible friendship was born.

At some point, Belle stepped up to the plinth again and

pulled the Fire Tiger out of the lock. Suddenly, there was a grinding sound under her feet. The plinth was gradually rising out of the floor.

"Jump up!" she called to the others, extending her hand towards Harold McFinnegan. Oni and Anubi, Connor and Oliver made it in time, too. The plinth was spiralling up higher and higher. Suddenly, the ceiling parted above them, into the temple's main chamber. They sailed past the black sedan chair and the altar, before the temple roof rumbled open, too. Their journey ended twenty metres above the jungle, right at the door of the Sky Explorer.

"Can't I leave you on your own even for an hour?" TICI greeted the teacher. "Your chances of survival will now increase by..."

"TICI," McFinnegan interrupted the AI device. "Your chances of not being switched off once and for all will increase by 100 per cent if you stop talking right now. Destination: Deep Fog Castle. And make it snappy!"

Special Status

Catherine Noir had set a new record with her Sky Divider so she could receive the unbelievable news in person. Now she was sitting in her office, with dishevelled hair and somewhat slapdash make-up, listening in awe to Belle Pompadour's words. Harry, the Komodo dragon, was lying at her feet, gnawing on a bone. Oliver didn't want to let him out of his sight for a moment.

Belle glossed over a few minor details in her report, and completely left out the fact they had stolen the Sky Explorer and broken the thoughtophone. But she did emphasise a number of times how everything had happened in an unplanned way, and how one event had led to another. At no point would it have been possible to report their findings to the experienced members of the ACE or ask them for help.

At the appropriate moment, Connor placed the Fire Tiger in front of Noir. Oni followed suit with the missing first part of the logbook, and Oliver with the construction drawing he had made of the autopilot on van Robbemond's ship. If the president were to doubt any word of their account, these artefacts would be proof of its truth.

When Belle had finished, Noir looked across at her old friend, Harold Godric McFinnegan.

"It was, well… just as Belle has described," he confirmed. "Van Robbemond has personally appointed these four as the custodians of the ACE."

Catherine Noir nodded. "Well, if van Robbemond has decided that, then it's not for me to go against his wishes," she said. "Rather, it is my duty to provide the appropriate support for all of this."

She looked at each of her pupils in turn. "You four will be given special status at the academy, but don't breathe a word about your custodianship of these magical artefacts to anyone. Not a soul may learn of your secret – no teacher, no pupil, not even Professor Maximov. After all, time and again we find elements within the ACE who tend more towards evil than good."

Connor, Oliver, Oni and Belle nodded.

"Harold will be your mentor and, if necessary, he will cover for you if you have any problems with the other teachers. Of course, I am also here if you need me. Do you understand?"

"You bet!" Oliver burst out. He pushed his glasses nervously up his nose. "I can play the whimpering nerd pretty well, can't I? Ow, ow, stop, Tyron, you're going to break my fingernail."

Everyone laughed.

"Your knowledge really helped us," Oni complimented him. "Except when you read wonderboots as 'wanderboots' – turns out, they were nothing to do with hiking! Eleven-Fingered Louie would never forgive you for that!"

Connor placed an approving hand on Belle's shoulder.

"The way you realised the tiger was the priestess – that was a stroke of genius," he said. "You saved us as well as the whole of humanity."

Belle laughed. "Since when have you given out compliments? Well, perhaps the Phantom will receive one in return… The way you pinched the dagger from the White Shadow while at the same time calling him dishonourable was second to none."

McFinnegan laughed drily.

"And Oni's gift saved our bacon quite a few times," Oliver gushed. "She even managed to pacify the enchanted tigress with it."

Belle beamed at her comrades – or rather, her friends. She put her arms around Oni and Oliver, and the two of them pulled Connor into the circle. Anubi climbed up to the spire on the tower and squealed in delight.

"Enough of all this flattery," Belle said, laughing. "Let's just agree on one thing: on our own we're remarkable, but together we're unbeatable!"

Catherine Noir was more than happy with the scene that was playing out in her office. Then she noticed Connor was peeking at the newspaper articles about the Phantom in her open drawer. Catherine Noir looked at Connor. He was an accomplished thief, a passionate fighter and a great freethinker, just like Bartholomeus van Robbemond, the founder of the ACE, his ancestor.

Had Connor worked this out already? Had he too noticed that he and van Robbemond had the same mole on his forearm? Like all the descendants of the founder of the ACE?

Smiling, Catherine Noir closed the drawer. "There's an opportunity in every crisis..." she muttered. She'd had plans for the Phantom. Some of these had been realised, some things had completely surprised her – and some things had been completely derailed. But that's just how it was with plans – usually, life got in the way.

But the next Adventure Academy of Europe expedition was bound to go more smoothly. She hoped…

Acknowledgements

I would like to thank the following people in particular:

Michael Mack for inventing the Adventure Club of Europe, and for his inexhaustible vision for the ACE.

The Mack family for the inspiring world of Europa-Park, which is full of fantastic adventures and brings the story of Bartholomeus van Robbemond and the Pirates in Batavia to life in incredible ways.

Nils Feigenwinter for his tireless commitment and the countless creative ideas that got the ACE Scouts and their Sky Explorer off the ground in the first place.

Jörg Ihle, Dominik Hochwald and Marcel Naas for steering this flight in the right direction.

Tobias Mundinger for his passion for getting the story of the ACE out to the world.

Anja Fislage and David Ginnuttis for the meticulousness and wisdom with which they solved many a plot hole, and for helping to breathe life into the characters.

$E = mc^2$
$S = a^2\sqrt{3}/4$
$a = \frac{\Delta v}{t}$

bookworm

Nerd

clever

OLIVER SNYDER

researcher and inventor

riddle cracker

tinkerer